Rebirth In The Fallout

"A story of survival, leadership, and hope in a shattered world."

Michael Pettit

Rebirth In The Fallout
© 2024 Michael Pettit

All rights reserved. No part of this book may be reproduced, distributed, or transmitted in any form or by any means, including photocopying, recording, or other electronic or mechanical methods, without the prior written permission of the author, except in the case of brief quotations embodied in critical reviews and certain other noncommercial uses permitted by copyright law.

For permission requests, write to the author at:
michael.pettit4106@gmail.com

This is a work of fiction. Names, characters, businesses, places, events, and incidents are either the products of the author's imagination or used in a fictitious manner. Any resemblance to actual persons, living or dead, or actual events is purely coincidental.

First Edition: 2024
ISBN: KDP 9798336039542

Independently published
Mooresville, NC

Cover Design by Harsh Ghanshya

Table of Contents

Chapter 1: The Final Hours 1

Chapter 2: The Day the World Ended 11

Chapter 3: The Bunker 22

Chapter 4: Emergence 31

Chapter 5: Command and Control 42

Chapter 6: The First Winter 50

Chapter 7: The Fragmented States 58

Chapter 8: Reclaiming the Capitol 65

Chapter 9: The Council of Reconciliation 71

Chapter 10: The Scavenger Missions 78

Chapter 11: The New Constitution 84

Chapter 12: Family Comes First 97

Chapter 13: The Rebellion 104

Chapter 14: The Legacy of War 115

Chapter 15: A Fragile Peace 122

Chapter 16: The New Military 128

Chapter 17: The New Dawn 135

Chapter 18: The Foreign Threat 148

Chapter 19: The Final Reckoning 158

Chapter 20: The Legacy of Leadership 168

Chapter 21: Rebirth 176

Chapter 1: The Final Hours

The Oval Office was a warm and quiet place, the sunshine breaking in through the large windows and making a colorful sunrise visible over Washington, D.C. The soft light was coming through the tall trees, causing big shadings to move into the space. President John Anderson was by the window, his hands held behind his back; he was lost in thought. The outside world was peaceful, but it did not seem so to him.

Reports of escalating global tensions had been arriving for weeks, each one more alarming than the last. The situation was deteriorating rapidly—diplomatic channels were closing, and the world seemed to be spiraling toward an abyss. John had spent countless hours in this very room, poring over intelligence briefings, holding late-night calls with foreign leaders, and consulting with his advisors. Despite their best efforts, the threat of nuclear war loomed larger every day.

"Mr. President, the National Security Council is ready for you," came the voice of Susan Ellis, his Chief of Staff. She stood at the doorway, her usually composed expression withered by worry. John turned away from the window, nodding to Susan as he gathered his thoughts. He had faced countless challenges during his presidency—economic crises, natural disasters, even acts of terrorism—but nothing compared to this. The possibility of nuclear war was a nightmare he had hoped to never confront. Yet here it was, staring him in the face.

As they walked down the corridor, the atmosphere was tense. Staff members moved with purpose, their expressions worrisome. The usually bustling halls were eerily quiet, as if everyone was holding their breath. John's footsteps echoed softly against the marble floors, each step a reminder of the heavy responsibility he bears.

When they reached the Situation Room, the air was thick with anticipation. The room was packed with his top advisors: the Secretary of Defense, the Director of the CIA, the Chairman of the Joint Chiefs of Staff, and other senior officials. They were already seated around the large table, their faces a mix of determination and dread. The digital screens on the walls displayed maps of the world, each one marked with flashing red indicators that signaled impending danger.

John took his seat at the head of the table, the weight of his role pressing down on him. He looked around at the faces of his advisors—people he trusted, people who had stood by him through countless crises. But even they seemed shaken by the gravity of the situation.

"Give me the latest," John said, his voice steady but with a feeling of worry.

The Director of National Intelligence was the first to speak, his tone somber. "Mr. President, we have confirmed that multiple hostile nations have mobilized their nuclear arsenals. Satellite imagery shows several missile silos being prepared for launch. We believe they are targeting major U.S. cities, including Washington, D.C., New York, Los Angeles, and Chicago."

John felt a cold chill run down his spine. The room was silent, the only sound was the soft hum of the tech around the room. He could sense the fear in the room, though no one dared voice it. The very thought of those cities—each one a symbol of American strength and culture—being reduced to ashes was unbearable.

"What are our options?" John asked, forcing himself to stay composed.

The Secretary of Defense leaned forward. "Sir, we have our own strategic forces on high alert. Our bombers are in the air, our submarines are ready, and our missile defense systems are activated. We can launch a preemptive strike to neutralize their capabilities, but such a move would almost certainly escalate the situation into full-scale nuclear war."

"And if we don't?" John's voice was quiet, but the question hung heavy in the air.

The Chairman of the Joint Chiefs spoke next, his tone direct. "Our missile defense systems are advanced, but they're not perfect. Some warheads will get through. If the enemy launches a full-scale attack, the damage to our cities and infrastructure will be catastrophic. We're talking about millions of lives lost, Mr. President."

John closed his eyes for a moment, trying to absorb the enormity of what he was hearing. Every decision he made in the next few minutes would shape the fate of the world. The lives of countless innocent people depended on him making the right call.

"Are there any diplomatic avenues left?" John asked, searching for even the slimmest chance of avoiding disaster.

Susan Ellis responded, her voice tinged with urgency. "Mr. President, we've reached out through every possible channel. We've offered concessions, pleaded for restraint, but we've received no response. The enemy seems determined to launch their attack."

A heavy silence fell over the room. The hope of a peaceful resolution was slipping away, replaced by the harsh reality of the situation. John knew that his options were limited—no matter what he chose, there would be dire consequences.

He stood up, his gaze sweeping across the room. "Prepare for the worst. But we will not initiate a strike unless we have confirmation that their missiles are in the air. I want every possible defense in place, and I want updates every minute."

His advisors are quick to their duties, understanding the gravity of the command. The room quickly became a hive of activity as orders were relayed and preparations began. John remained standing, watching as his team moved with purpose. He knew they were doing everything they could, but the feeling of helplessness gnawed at him.

Minutes passed, each one feeling like an eternity. John watched the digital map on the screen, the red markers indicating missile silos and launch sites. The tension in the room was palpable, everyone waiting for the inevitable.

Then, the dreaded confirmation came. A staff member at the communications desk stood up, his face pale. "Mr. President, we have confirmation—multiple missiles have been launched. They're on a direct course for the United States."

The words hung in the air like a death sentence. The room erupted into controlled chaos, with advisors barking orders, military officials coordinating defenses, and intelligence analysts tracking the missile trajectories. John felt a surge of adrenaline, his mind racing as he tried to process the reality of what was happening.

He could see the paths of the missiles on the screen, arcing across the globe toward American soil. Each trajectory represented a city, a community, a piece of the nation he had sworn to protect. The thought of those places—filled with people going about their daily lives, unaware of the horror speeding toward them—was almost too much to bear.

"Mr. President, we need to get you to the bunker," Susan's voice cut through the din, bringing him back to the present.

His movements feeling almost automatic. He knew that staying above ground was no longer an option—the White House was a primary target. As he followed Susan and a group of Secret Service agents through the corridors, the reality of the situation hit him with full force. The city he loved, the capital of the nation, was about to be engulfed in nuclear fire.

The wail of sirens filled the air as they approached the bunker entrance. The sirens, a sound that had been tested so many times in drills, now had a terrifying urgency. The streets outside would be filled with people scrambling for shelter, their fear and confusion echoing in the chaos.

As they reached the heavy steel doors of the bunker, John took one last look at the White House. The iconic building stood proud against the backdrop of the brightening sky, a symbol of American resilience and democracy. But he knew that within minutes, it would likely be reduced to rubble.

The doors sealed shut behind him with a resounding thud, cutting him off from the world above. The bunker was a stark, cold space—designed for survival, not comfort. John felt the weight of the moment pressing down on him, the enormity of what was happening nearly overwhelming.

Inside the bunker, the Situation Room was replicated, except on a smaller scale. Monitors displayed the incoming missile trajectories, while a constant stream of data flowed in from military and intelligence sources. The tension was suffocating, every person in the room knowing that the world outside was about to change forever.

John sank into a chair, feeling the exhaustion catch up to him. He knew there was no more he could do but wait. The fate of the nation, of the world, was no longer in his hands. It was in the hands of the military personnel trying to intercept the missiles, in the systems designed to protect against such an attack. But he couldn't shake the feeling that it was all futile—that no defense could stop what was coming.

Minutes passed like hours as they watched the screens. The first explosions were detected on the West Coast. A massive fireball engulfed Los Angeles, followed by San Francisco. Reports of total devastation began flooding in—communications cut off, entire cities vaporized in seconds.

And then, the ground beneath them shook. The shockwave from Washington, D.C. detonation reached the bunker, a rumbling that reverberated through the earth. The power flickered for a moment before the backup generators kicked in, casting the room in a dim, eerie glow.

John closed his eyes, the enormity of the loss weighing heavily on him. He pictured the streets of Washington, now likely reduced to smoldering ruins. The monuments, the museums, the neighborhoods—all gone in an instant. And with them, the heart of the nation.

When he opened his eyes again, the screens showed the aftermath—a world plunged into chaos, with cities across the country in ruins. The United States, the superpower that had once stood as a beacon of hope, was now a shattered remnant of its former self.

John knew that his role as President had not ended with the strike. If anything, his duty was only beginning. He would have to lead what remained of the country through the most challenging time in its history. The task ahead seemed impossible, but he had no choice. He had to find a way to rebuild, to restore hope in a world where everything had been lost.

Chapter 2: The Day the World Ended

The bunker's walls, thick and cold, pressed in around the President as he stared at the array of monitors flickering in the dim light. The sterile air, recycled and stale, did little to ease the tension that clung to every corner of the room. His heart pounded with a mix of adrenaline and dread. The enormity of the disaster that had just unfolded was beyond comprehension. The world above was gone, consumed by fire and radiation, but here in the depths of the Earth, the remnants of a government clung to life.

John sat at the head of the conference table, surrounded by his most trusted advisors. The weight of their collective silence was crushing, each of them grappling with the same realization: the world they knew had been irrevocably shattered.

"Damage assessments are coming in now, Mr. President," said General Adam Moore, the Chairman of the Joint Chiefs of Staff. His voice, usually commanding and resolute, wavered slightly as he delivered the harsh news. He held a tablet in his hands, the glow of the screen casting a harsh light on his weathered face. "We've lost contact with most of the major cities on the East Coast. Washington, D.C., New York, Boston… they're gone. The West Coast was hit hard as well—Los Angeles, San Francisco, Seattle. Casualties are in the millions, sir."

John felt the words hit him like a physical blow, each city name conjuring images of the vibrant life that had once filled those streets. He imagined the bustling sidewalks of New York, the iconic skyline now reduced to rubble. The halls of power in Washington, D.C., where just hours ago, he had been making decisions in the Oval Office, now a smoldering ruin. The thought of all those lives—millions of people, families, children—snuffed out in an instant was almost too much to bear.

"What about our forces?" John forced himself to ask, his voice tight. He had to stay focused on the task at hand, no matter how overwhelming it felt. There was still a country to lead, however broken it might be.

General Moore straightened, slipping back into the familiar role of a soldier delivering a report. "Our strategic forces are still intact, Mr. President, but we've taken heavy losses. Several key military bases were targeted in the initial strikes, and we've lost contact with our command centers in those regions. Our communications network is severely compromised. We're struggling to coordinate with remaining units across the country. Many of our systems are either down or operating at minimal capacity."

John absorbed the words being spoken though his mind was racing. The military, the backbone of the nation's defense, was crippled. Without a clear chain of command and reliable communication, the country was vulnerable to further attacks, or worse, complete societal collapse. The room seemed to shrink around him, the air thick with the magnitude of the situation.

"Radiation levels?" John asked, his voice quieter now. He knew the answer wouldn't be good, but he had to hear it anyway.

Dr. Emily Kline, the President's Science Advisor, sat to his right, her hands trembling slightly as she scrolled through data on her tablet. She was a brilliant scientist, her expertise in environmental and nuclear sciences unparalleled, but even she seemed at a loss for words. "Mr. President, the radiation levels are… catastrophic. The fallout from the blasts is spreading rapidly across the country, carried by the winds. The initial impact zones are, of course, unsurvivable, but we're now seeing lethal radiation levels extending hundreds of miles from those sites. Major population centers that weren't directly hit by the blasts are still in grave danger."

She paused, swallowing hard before continuing. "Those who survived the initial strikes are now at risk of radiation sickness. Without immediate medical intervention, they won't last long. The infrastructure to deal with such widespread contamination doesn't exist anymore. We're looking at potentially millions more deaths in the coming days and weeks."

John felt a deep, gnawing fear take hold of him. The fallout was like an invisible death creeping across the country, sparing no one in its path. He thought of the people—those who had managed to find shelter, those who were huddled in basements and makeshift bunkers, praying that they might survive the next few hours. But survival wasn't guaranteed, not when the very air they breathed could kill them.

"What about the rest of the world?" John asked, knowing that the impact of the nuclear strikes would not be confined to American soil. The interconnected nature of the world meant that no nation would be untouched by the disaster.

Secretary of State Tammy Blair, usually poised and unflappable, looked visibly shaken as she spoke. Her voice was a low murmur, as if she were reluctant to share the news. "It's… bad, Mr. President. The strikes weren't limited to the United States. Our intelligence indicates that multiple NATO allies in Europe have been hit—London, Paris, Berlin… all targeted. We're also receiving reports of strikes in Russia and China. It appears that their major cities and military sites have been targeted as well. The Middle East, Asia, and even parts of Africa have been affected. This wasn't just a regional conflict—it's a global catastrophe."

John closed his eyes, the weight of her words nearly crushing him. The world had been thrust into a nuclear apocalypse. The global order, built over decades of careful diplomacy, strategic alliances, and economic interdependence, had collapsed in a matter of hours. Billions of lives across the planet were either lost or in immediate peril. He thought of the world's great cities, now likely nothing more than radioactive craters, and the centuries of human progress wiped out in an instant.

He opened his eyes and looked around the room. His advisors, his trusted staff, were all grappling with the same horrifying reality. But despite the fear etched on their faces, he saw a spark of determination in each of them. They were waiting for him, their leader, to guide them through the nightmare.

"We need to establish a clear chain of command," John said, his voice firm despite the despair that threatened to overwhelm him. "General Moore, I need you to take charge of coordinating our remaining military forces. We need to secure whatever resources we have left and protect the survivors. Communications are our top priority—without them, we're blind. I want every available resource directed toward re-establishing contact with our forces and what remains of the government."

General Moore agreed, already tapping out orders on his tablet. "Yes, Mr. President. We'll do everything we can to restore communications and regroup our forces. We still have some assets in place—our nuclear submarines, for instance, are still operational. They'll be a key part of our strategy moving forward."

John turned to Secretary Blair. "Blair, continue reaching out to our allies, and try to establish some kind of global coordination. We need to know who's still standing and what resources they have. If there's any chance of a coordinated response, we have to take it. The world won't survive if we all go at it alone."

Blair's lips pressed into a thin line as she was writing out her orders. "I'll do everything I can, sir. But it's going to be difficult. Most of our traditional communication networks are down, and the few that are still operational are overloaded with traffic. It's hard to get a clear picture of what's happening globally. And with so many of our key allies in chaos… I'm not sure how many of them are even in a position to respond."

John acknowledged her words with a nod of his head. He knew the chances of a coordinated global effort were slim, but they had to try. In the face of such unprecedented destruction, any hope, no matter how faint, had to be pursued.

"Dr. Kline," John said, turning to his Science Advisor, "we need to assess the environmental damage and figure out how to protect the survivors from the fallout. Is there any way to create safe zones—areas where the radiation is less severe? We need places where people can go, where they have a chance of surviving."

Kline hesitated, her face pale as she considered the enormity of the task. "Mr. President, the radiation levels are fluctuating, and it's difficult to predict where the fallout will settle. But it might be possible to identify areas with natural barriers—mountain ranges, dense forests, places where the geography might offer some protection. We could also look at existing infrastructure—underground facilities, old military bunkers, things like that. But the resources to establish and maintain these zones are limited, especially with our current situation."

"I understand," John replied, his tone resolute. "But we have to try. I want you to work with the military to identify potential sites and start making plans. We need to give people somewhere to go, somewhere to survive. It's the only way we can hold onto any kind of order."

Kline's features hardened, filled with determination. "I'll get to work on it right away, Mr. President. But we're going to need every available resource—medical supplies, food, clean water, radiation suits. If we don't move fast, the death toll could skyrocket."

John's heart sank as he imagined the dark future that lay ahead. The survivors, already traumatized by the devastation they'd witnessed, would face a world where even the basics of survival were scarce. Disease, hunger, and radiation sickness would stalk the land, claiming lives in numbers that defied comprehension.

As he sat there, the enormity of his task pressed down on him like a physical weight. The United States, once the beacon of hope and power in the world, was now a wasteland. But as long as he drew breath, John knew he couldn't give up. The people who had survived were counting on him to lead them through the darkness, to find a way to rebuild even from the ashes.

"Ladies and gentlemen," John said, his voice steady and filled with resolve, "this is the darkest moment in our history. But we cannot give in to despair. We owe it to the survivors, to those who didn't make it, to do everything in our power to rebuild. This country, this world, it's not finished yet. We'll face unimaginable challenges in the days ahead, but we will face them together. We will endure. We must."

His words hung in the air, a fragile beacon of hope in a sea of despair. Around the table, his advisors straightened in their seats, their expressions shifting from fear to determination. They had lost so much, but as long as they were alive, there was still a chance to fight back, to reclaim some small part of what had been lost.

John leaned back in his chair, the weight of the presidency heavier than ever before. He knew that the road ahead would be long and fraught with peril, but he was determined to lead his people through the nightmare that had engulfed them. They would rebuild, one step at a time, even if it meant starting from nothing.

As the bunker settled into an uneasy quiet, John took a deep breath, bracing himself for what was to come. The world outside was a wasteland, but within these walls, there was still life, still hope. And as long as there was hope, there was a reason to fight.

Chapter 3: The Bunker

The hum of the bunker's ventilation system was the only constant sound in the President's quarters. It was a low, steady noise that would have been soothing under different circumstances, but now, it only amplified the eerie silence that filled the room. The walls, thick and reinforced, seemed to close in around him, making the space feel more like a tomb than a sanctuary.

John sat at the small desk in the corner of the room, staring at a blank piece of paper. A pen rested in his hand, but he couldn't bring himself to write. What was there to say? The words that used to flow so easily now felt trapped inside him, buried under the weight of everything that had happened. He had always prided himself on his ability to lead, to inspire, but now, he felt lost.

The bunker's harsh fluorescent lighting cast long shadows across the room, accentuating the starkness of his surroundings. There were no personal touches here, no photographs, no mementos from his life before the war. Everything had been left behind in the mad rush to reach safety. His family, his home, his entire world—it was all gone, replaced by this cold, sterile environment. The realization struck him again with a fresh wave of grief. Where were they? Were they safe? The not knowing was a constant gnawing at his insides, a wound that wouldn't heal.

He closed his eyes and tried to remember the last time he had seen them. It had been just a few days ago, though it felt like a lifetime. They had been in the White House, going about their daily routines. His wife, Katherine, had been reading a book in the living room, her glasses perched on the end of her nose. Their two children, Emily and Bryan, had been playing in the garden, their laughter filling the air. It was a moment of normalcy; one he had taken for granted.

And now... what? Were they still alive? Had they found shelter? The questions circled endlessly in his mind, each one more torturous than the last. He had sent them to a secure location as soon as the situation had escalated, but the chaos of those final hours before the bombs fell made everything a blur. Communications had been severed, and in the chaos, he had lost contact with them. The thought of them out there, possibly alone and afraid, was almost too much to bear.

John leaned forward, resting his head in his hands. The overwhelming grief threatened to consume him, but he fought to keep it at bay. He had to stay focused. There was still so much to do, so many decisions to make. The country was in ruins, and its people were depending on him to lead them through this nightmare. He couldn't afford to break down now.

A sharp knock on the door pulled him from his thoughts. He sat up quickly, taking a deep breath to steady himself. "Come in," he called, his voice hoarse from disuse.

The door opened, and Vice President Karen Brooks stepped inside. She moved with a quiet grace, her expression a mix of concern and determination. Karen had always been a strong presence in his administration, someone he could rely on without question. She had been by his side through countless challenges, but nothing had prepared them for this.

"Mr. President," Karen said softly, closing the door behind her. She hesitated for a moment, as if unsure whether to approach. "I hope I'm not interrupting."

John shook his head, forcing a small smile. "Not at all, Karen. I'm glad you're here."

Karen took a seat across from him, her eyes scanning his face. She could see the exhaustion, the grief, etched into his face. "How are you holding up, John?" she asked, her voice gentle.

John let out a long breath, leaning back in his chair. "I don't know," he admitted. "I keep thinking about... everything. The people we've lost, the destruction... it's hard to wrap my head around it all. And my family..." His voice broke slightly, and he had to pause to collect himself. "I don't even know if they're alive, Karen."

Karen reached out, placing a hand on his arm. "We'll find them, John. I know it feels impossible right now, but we'll find them. You have to hold on to that hope."

John bowed his head. "I'm trying, but it's hard. Everything we've known is gone. How do we even begin to move forward?"

Karen's expression hardened with resolve. "We do it one step at a time. We can't dwell on what we've lost, John. We have to focus on what we can do, on the people who are still alive and need us. This country is in chaos, but it's not finished. As long as we're still here, there's hope."

John admired Karen's strength. She had always been the more practical of the two, able to keep a clear head even in the most trying circumstances. It was a quality that had served them well during their time in office, and one that would be invaluable now.

"I've been thinking about what comes next," John said, shifting the conversation to the practical matters at hand. "We've talked about securing resources and establishing safe zones, but we also need to think about leadership. The government is in shambles, and people are going to be looking to us for guidance. We need to rebuild some sort of order, or we'll lose what little stability we have left."

Karen, her mind already working through the logistics. "You're right. We can't afford to be reactive—we need a plan. We'll need to establish a clear chain of command, not just for the military, but for civilian authorities as well. We'll need to delegate responsibilities, empower regional leaders, and start thinking about how to re-establish some form of communication with the public."

John leaned forward, considering her words. "It's going to be a monumental task, especially with our infrastructure in ruins. But we can't do it alone. We'll need to rely on whoever's left in the government—state governors, mayors, anyone with the ability to lead."

"Agreed," Karen replied. "We also need to reach out to the people. They need to know that their government hasn't abandoned them, that we're still here, fighting for them. It's going to be difficult, but it's essential if we're going to maintain any kind of order."

John now feels a renewed sense of purpose. "We'll start working on it immediately. I'll need your help to coordinate with the remaining government officials, and we'll need to start drafting a plan for how we're going to communicate with the public."

Karen smiled, though it was tinged with sadness. "You've got it, John. We'll figure this out together, just like we always have."

They sat in silence for a moment, both of them reflecting on the enormity of the task ahead. The world outside the bunker was a wasteland, but within these walls, there was still hope. It was fragile, easily extinguished, but as long as they were alive, there was a chance to rebuild, to restore some semblance of what had been lost.

"I've been thinking about our priorities," John said after a long pause. "We need to focus on survival first—securing food, water, and medical supplies. But we also need to start thinking about the long term. We have to find a way to rebuild, to create a new society out of the ashes of the old one."

Karen's expression turned serious. "It's going to be a long, hard road, John. But I believe we can do it. We've faced impossible odds before, and we've come through. This is different, of course, but we can't give up. We owe it to the people who are still out there, fighting to survive."

John felt a surge of gratitude for Karen's unwavering support. She had always been his rock, and now, in the darkest of times, she was there to help him find his way. "Thank you, Karen," he said, his voice thick with emotion. "I don't know what I'd do without you."

Karen reached across the table, placing her hand over his. "We're in this together, John. We always have been, and we always will be."

As Karen left the room, John felt a strange mix of emotions—grief for the world they had lost, but also a glimmer of hope for the future. They were standing on the edge of the abyss, but they hadn't fallen in. Not yet. There was still a chance to pull back, to find a way to survive and rebuild.

But as he sat alone in the quiet of his quarters, John couldn't shake the feeling that the worst was yet to come. The world was a different place now, filled with dangers they couldn't even begin to comprehend. They had survived the initial onslaught, but the struggle was far from over.

For now, though, he would take it one step at a time. He had to. The future of the nation, the world, depended on it.

Chapter 4: Emergence

The bunker had been their sanctuary for weeks, a place where the remnants of the U.S. government had sheltered from the horrors above. But the air inside had grown stale, not just from the recycled oxygen, but from the weight of what lay beyond the thick steel doors. Every day spent underground was a reminder of the world that had been lost—and of the world they needed to rebuild.

The President stood in the command center, surrounded by monitors and maps that offered a glimpse of the devastation outside. His hands rested on the edge of a large table, his fingers tracing the outline of the United States as it appeared now—scarred, fragmented, but still recognizable. The time had come to leave the bunker, to face the new reality head-on.

"Mr. President," General Moore said, breaking the heavy silence. The general, a man whose calm demeanor belied the turmoil of the last few weeks, approached with a determined stride. "The team is ready. The scouts have reported that the radiation levels have dropped to a survivable level in the immediate area. It's still dangerous, but we can't afford to wait any longer."

John agreed, his resolve hardening. They had planned for this moment, but now that it was here, the enormity of it weighed heavily on him. "What about transportation?" he asked, his voice steady.

"We've managed to secure a few operational vehicles," Moore replied. "They're equipped with radiation shielding and enough fuel to get us to the nearest safe zone. We'll also be taking one of the helicopters for aerial reconnaissance and emergency evacuation if needed."

Karen, entered the room carrying a small pack of personal belongings—barely more than what could fit in a single bag. She glanced at John, her eyes filled with a mixture of determination and concern. "Are we really ready for this?" she asked quietly.

"We have to be," John replied, his tone firm but not unkind. "We've spent too long underground. If we're going to lead the country through this, we need to see the reality for ourselves."

Karen understood the necessity even as the anxiety gnawed at her. They had all heard the reports, seen the satellite images, but nothing could prepare them for what awaited above.

John turned to Moore. "Make sure the teams know the plan. We move quickly, secure the area, and establish a new base of operations topside. We need to find survivors, re-establish communication, and start rebuilding."

Moore saluted sharply. "Yes, Mr. President."

With that, the preparations began in earnest. Soldiers and staff members moved with purpose, gathering supplies, checking equipment, and double-checking their plans. The atmosphere in the bunker was electric, charged with the knowledge that they were about to step into a world that had been irrevocably altered.

John took a moment to look around the command center, his gaze lingering on the people who had become his family in the weeks since the bombs fell. These were the ones who had kept the flame of government alive, who had worked tirelessly to keep some semblance of order in a world plunged into chaos. And now they were about to embark on the most critical mission of their lives.

"Mr. President," Karen said, her voice soft but firm. "We're ready."

John is feeling the weight of the moment settle on his shoulders. He took a deep breath, steeling himself for what lay ahead. "Let's go."

The heavy doors of the bunker groaned as they slowly slid open, revealing a sliver of the outside world—a world that had been obliterated by nuclear fire and now lay in ruins. A sharp, acrid smell immediately assaulted John's senses, a potent mix of burnt earth, smoke, and decay. It was the first time in months that he had smelled anything other than the sterile air of the bunker, and it hit him like a punch to the gut. The world outside was no longer the one they had left behind.

John stood at the threshold, a mix of dread and determination tightening his chest. Behind him, his small team of soldiers and key advisors waited in tense silence, their faces pale but resolute. General Moore, ever the stoic figure, stood at his side, ready to lead them into whatever awaited beyond the bunker's protection.

"This is it," John said, his voice steady despite the knot in his stomach. "We've prepared for this, but nothing can fully prepare us for what we're about to see. Remember, our mission is clear: establish a new base of operations and begin the process of rebuilding. We do this for everyone who didn't make it, and for those who are still out there."

General Moore's eyes locked on the barren landscape ahead. "We'll move quickly and keep a low profile. The roads will be treacherous, but our vehicles are ready. We need to get to that outpost before nightfall."

With a final glance back at the bunker—a place that had kept them safe but had also become their prison—John took the first step outside. The ground beneath his boots was uneven, a mix of cracked pavement and debris from the world that had once been. The sky above was a dull, smoky gray, with thick clouds of ash obscuring the sun. It cast an eerie, perpetual twilight over the land, a constant reminder of the devastation that had been wrought.

The convoy was small but well-prepared: two armored trucks, each reinforced to withstand low levels of radiation and equipped with enough supplies to sustain them for the journey. Behind them, the bunker doors began to close, sealing off the subterranean refuge that had been their home for so long.

As the trucks rumbled to life, John climbed into the lead vehicle, settling into the passenger seat next to the driver, a young soldier whose face was set in determination. Karen, and General Moore joined them in the back, their presence a comforting reminder of the continuity of leadership, even in the face of unimaginable loss.

The convoy moved out, the tires crunching over the broken remnants of the road as they left the bunker behind. The world outside was a landscape of desolation. The once-thriving forests that had surrounded the area were now charred skeletons of trees, their blackened branches reaching up like twisted fingers. The air was thick with the remnants of the apocalypse—ash, dust, and a lingering sense of despair that clung to everything.

John stared out the window, his mind racing as he tried to process the scene before him. The last images he had seen of the world were from satellite feeds and grainy reconnaissance photos, but those had not captured the true scale of the destruction. Entire towns were gone, reduced to nothing but craters and rubble. The infrastructure that had once connected the country was shattered—roads cracked and buckled, bridges collapsed into the rivers they once spanned.

"Mr. President," Karen said softly, breaking the heavy silence that had settled over the group. "Do you think anyone could have survived this?"

John took a deep breath before answering. "We have to believe there are survivors out there, Karen. People are resilient. They would have found ways to protect themselves, to hold on. Our job is to find them, but first, we need to secure a base of operations. We can't help anyone if we're not in a position of strength."

General Moore, who had been scanning a map spread across his lap, added, "The outpost is in a remote area, far enough from any major city that it likely avoided the worst of the attacks. It's still intact, according to the last recon reports. Once we're there, we can assess our situation and begin planning our next moves."

As the convoy wound its way through the desolate landscape, the enormity of their task weighed heavily on John. Every mile brought new scenes of destruction—collapsed buildings, scorched earth, and the occasional husk of a vehicle abandoned in the chaos. Yet, amidst the devastation, there was a strange, unsettling beauty to the world. The silence was profound, almost deafening, broken only by the low rumble of the trucks and the occasional distant crack of shifting rubble.

They passed through what had once been a small town, now little more than a ghostly ruin. The town's welcome sign lay toppled on the ground, half-buried in dust and debris. The buildings, once homes and businesses filled with life, were now hollow shells, their windows shattered, their walls crumbling. John could almost picture the people who had lived here, going about their daily lives, completely unaware of the horror that was about to befall them.

"Keep moving," John instructed the driver, his voice barely above a whisper. He couldn't afford to dwell on the past—not now. There would be time to mourn later, time to remember all that had been lost. But for now, they had to focus on survival.

The road ahead became increasingly treacherous as they neared their destination. The once-paved highway had given way to rough, uneven terrain, with deep cracks and fissures cutting across the path. The driver maneuvered the truck carefully, avoiding the worst of the obstacles, but it was slow going.

As the sun began to dip toward the horizon, casting long shadows across the landscape, they finally caught sight of the outpost. It was a small, secluded military installation nestled in a valley, surrounded by hills that had shielded it from the worst of the blasts. The perimeter fence was still intact, and the buildings within showed no signs of significant damage. It was a beacon of hope in a world that had been stripped of it.

"Looks like the recon team was right," Moore said, relief evident in his voice. "The outpost is still standing."

John felt a surge of relief, tempered by the knowledge that their journey was far from over. "Let's get inside and secure the perimeter. We need to assess the situation and make sure it's safe before we settle in."

The convoy rolled through the gates, which creaked as they swung open. Inside, the base was eerily quiet, the only sounds being those of their own movements and the distant whirr of the helicopter overhead. The outpost had been abandoned in the rush to evacuate when the bombs fell, but it was remarkably well-preserved. The buildings were sturdy, built to withstand attacks, and the storage facilities were stocked with supplies—food, water, medical equipment, and fuel.

John stepped out of the truck, taking in the sight of the base. It wasn't much, but it was something—a place to start. The others began unloading the trucks, their movements quick and efficient despite the fatigue that weighed on them.

As they worked, John felt a glimmer of hope. This was the first step, the beginning of their long road to recovery. The outpost would serve as their new headquarters, a place from which they could begin the arduous task of rebuilding the nation.

"We've made it this far," John said, gathering his team around him. "But this is just the beginning. The road ahead will be long and difficult, but we're not just survivors—we're the foundation of a new beginning. We have a duty to each other, to those who are still out there, and to the future of our country. We will rebuild, and we will endure. Together."

His words echoed through the quiet base, a rallying cry that cut through the despair and uncertainty. As the lights flickered on, casting a warm glow over the faces of those who had survived to see this moment, John felt a renewed sense of purpose. This was their world now, and it was up to them to shape its future.

Chapter 5: Command and Control

The air inside the command center was thick with tension, every breath a reminder of the enormity of the task ahead. John stood at the center of the room, surrounded by the hum of machinery and the low murmurs of his team as they worked tirelessly to bring the base's communication systems back online. Outside, the world lay in ruins, but within these walls, the future of the nation was being forged.

The first step was re-establishing communication with any surviving military bases and state leaders. Without a clear line of command, chaos would continue to reign. The Vice President, was at the helm of this effort, her fingers flying across a keyboard as she worked to scan for any surviving networks. The base's equipment was old and battered, the systems prone to failure, but Karen had been in tougher spots before. She was relentless in her determination.

"Anything yet?" John asked, his voice low but urgent.

Karen didn't look up, her focus entirely on the screen in front of her. "We've managed to establish a weak connection with a few military satellites. I'm trying to boost the signal now. If we're lucky, we might be able to reach some of the more remote bases that could have survived the initial blasts."

John's heart pounded in his chest. Every second that ticked by without contact was another second of uncertainty. The government had been decimated, the chain of command shattered, but if they could find even one other base, one other leader, they could start to piece things back together.

A burst of static crackled through the speakers, causing everyone in the room to freeze. Karen's fingers moved faster, adjusting the frequency, her eyes narrowing as she strained to make sense of the garbled transmission.

"This is Fort Bragg…repeat…Fort Bragg…copy?"

The voice was faint, barely discernible through the interference, but it was there. A lifeline in the darkness. John stepped closer, his breath catching in his throat. "This is President Anderson. Do you copy?"

There was a long pause, filled only by the hiss of static, before the voice came through again, clearer this time. "Mr. President…this is Colonel Thompson at Fort Bragg. We copy. What are your orders, sir?"

John closed his eyes, the weight of the moment pressing down on him. They had found a survivor, a military base that had withstood the destruction. It was a small victory, but a victory, nonetheless. "Colonel, we're working to re-establish communications with other surviving bases and state leaders. We need to coordinate rescue and relief efforts for any civilian populations that might still be out there. What's your status?"

"Fort Bragg took heavy damage, sir," Thompson replied. "We've lost a lot of good people, but we're holding. Supplies are low, and we've got wounded, but we're operational. We'll do whatever we can to assist."

"We're going to need every resource we can muster Colonel" John said, his mind already racing with the possibilities. "We will be sending a convoy to your location, any extra supplies or soldiers to spare are to load up on to the convoy" Thompson replied "Yes sir, over and out."

As the connection was secured, John turned to Karen, who was already working to establish contact with other potential survivors. Her face was pale, exhaustion etched into every line, but she didn't stop. She couldn't. Not when so much was at stake.

"We're getting reports from other state leaders," she said, her voice tight with concentration. "Some are just as scattered as we are—local governments trying to maintain order, but it's chaos out there, John. People are scared, desperate. They're looking for leadership, and if we don't give it to them…"

"They'll tear each other apart," John finished with his voice barely above a whisper. He knew she was right. In the vacuum left by the collapse of the federal government, power struggles were inevitable. Local leaders would try to assert control, militias might rise, and the fabric of society could unravel completely.

They needed to act quickly. "Karen, get me a list of all surviving state leaders. We need to establish a clear line of authority, even if it's temporary. We'll work with whoever is still out there, but we have to show that the federal government is still standing, still capable of leading."

Karen acknowledged this and went back to work. Meanwhile, John turned to General Moore, who had been overseeing the base's security and supply distribution. The general's face was lined with fatigue, but his eyes were sharp, assessing the situation with the calm efficiency that had become his hallmark.

"General, we need to start organizing rescue and relief efforts," John said. "There are survivors out there—civilians who need our help. We can't just focus on the military. We have to be the lifeline for everyone who's still hanging on."

Moore is unsure with his expression grim. "It's going to be tough, Mr. President. The infrastructure is in shambles, and we don't have the manpower to cover the entire country. But we'll do what we can. I'll start coordinating with Fort Bragg and any other bases we manage to contact. We'll prioritize the most densely populated areas first—anywhere that might still have significant numbers of survivors."

The challenge was immense, and John knew it. The roads were damaged or destroyed, radiation pockets made entire regions impassable, and the few remaining resources were spread thin. But they had to try. Every life they could save was another piece of the country's future.

As the hours passed, the scope of the devastation became clearer. Reports trickled in from state leaders and military outposts. Entire cities had been wiped off the map, vast swathes of the country rendered uninhabitable. The death toll was unimaginable, and the number of survivors dwindled with each passing day. The morale of those who remained at the base was fragile, teetering on the edge of despair.

In the privacy of his office, John stared at the list of names on his desk—names of the dead, of the missing, of those he had sworn to protect. He knew that he had to keep morale up, to inspire hope where there was little to be found. But how could he do that when the future was so uncertain?

Karen knocked softly on the door, breaking him from his thoughts. She stepped inside, her face drawn but determined. "We've managed to establish contact with several more bases, and a few governors are still in power.

They're looking to you, John. They want to know what the plan is."

John pushed aside his doubts. "We'll start with the basics. Stabilize the areas we can reach, coordinate relief efforts, and get the infrastructure back online where possible. We'll need to set up temporary governments if necessary—give people something to hold onto, a sense of normalcy."

Karen studied him for a moment, her eyes searching his. "You're doing the best you can, John. We all are. But this…this is bigger than any of us. We have to be prepared for the fact that we might not be able to save everyone."

He knew she was right, but that didn't make it any easier. "We'll save as many as we can, Karen. And we'll rebuild, one step at a time. But we have to keep going. We can't let despair win."

She agreed, her expression softening. "We won't. Not as long as you're leading us."

As she left the room, John felt a renewed sense of purpose. The challenges they faced were immense, and the road ahead was fraught with danger and uncertainty. But they had taken the first step—they had re-established contact, begun to organize, and started the process of rebuilding.

The nation had been brought to its knees, but it was not defeated. Not yet. And as long as there were people willing to fight for it, there was still hope.

John sat down at his desk, pulling out his notebook and flipping to a fresh page. He wrote down the words that had been guiding him since the day the bombs fell: *Rebuild, Restore, Recover.* And beneath it, he added a new word: *Endure.*

Chapter 6: The First Winter

The first snowfall came earlier than expected. It started as a light dusting, a thin veil of white that covered the ground like a shroud. But within hours, it had grown into a relentless blizzard, the wind howling through the skeletal remains of trees and whipping against the walls of the base. The world outside was a frozen wasteland, as if the earth itself had given up and succumbed to the cold embrace of death.

Inside the base, the atmosphere was just as bleak. The harsh winter, compounded by the nuclear fallout, made survival even more precarious. The frigid temperatures seeped into every crack and crevice, making the already difficult conditions unbearable. John stood by a small window in the command center, watching as the snow piled up against the fences and covered the remains of the outside world. The cold bit at his skin, even through the layers of clothing he wore, but it was nothing compared to the chill that had settled in his heart.

Supplies were dwindling. The food rations were being stretched thinner by the day, and the water supplies were dangerously low. The radiation had poisoned many natural sources, leaving them with few options. And shelter—real, adequate shelter—was becoming increasingly difficult to provide as more survivors were found and brought to the base. The once-mighty installation now felt like a prison, its walls closing in as the desperation grew.

General Moore had taken charge of the resource distribution efforts, but the task was nothing but stressful. The base was never meant to sustain this many people for so long, and every decision was a matter of life and death. The rationing was strict, and every morsel of food, every drop of water, was carefully calculated. But even the most meticulous planning couldn't change the fact that they were running out of everything.

In the mess hall, where the survivors gathered to eat their meager meals, the mood was somber. The once-strong soldiers now moved with a weariness that came from more than just physical exhaustion. The civilians who had been brought in were gaunt, their eyes hollow with hunger and fear. The food, which had once been just enough to sustain them, was now barely a whisper of sustenance. Each day, the rations grew smaller, and each day, the tension in the air grew thicker.

John knew that the administration's efforts to distribute resources were crucial, but no matter how much they tried to ensure fairness, it was impossible to ignore the fact that there simply wasn't enough to go around. The realization weighed heavily on him, a constant reminder of the gravity of his decisions. He had promised to lead, to protect, and to rebuild, but as the days grew colder and the supplies dwindled, those promises felt like a cruel joke.

Karen, ever the resilient force in his administration, was in the thick of the resource management efforts. She coordinated with General Moore, working to ensure that every resource was maximized, that nothing was wasted. But even she couldn't hide the strain it was taking on her. The lines on her face had deepened, her shoulders slumped under the weight of the responsibility they all shared.

"We need to find more supplies," Karen said one evening as they sat in John's small office, a map of the surrounding area spread out before them. "We can't keep this up much longer. The people are already on edge, and if we don't do something soon…"

John leaned back in his chair, rubbing a hand over his tired eyes. The thought of sending out more teams into the freezing wasteland, risking lives for the slim chance of finding untainted food or water, filled him with dread. But what choice did they have? "We'll have to risk it. There's no other way."

Karen nodded, though her expression was worrisome. "We'll need to be careful. The storms are getting worse, and the radiation levels are unpredictable. But if we don't try, we're condemning everyone here to a slow death."

John didn't respond immediately. Instead, he stared at the map, his mind racing with the possibilities—and the consequences. He knew the risks, knew that every decision he made could mean the difference between life and death for the people under his care. The weight of that responsibility was crushing, and it was taking its toll on him.

At night, when the base was quiet and the darkness closed in around him, John's thoughts turned inward. The guilt gnawed at him, a constant presence that he couldn't shake.

He had made it out of the bunker, had survived when so many hadn't, and now he was expected to lead the remnants of a shattered nation. But what kind of leader was he, really? Was he making the right choices? Was he doing enough?

He thought of the faces of the survivors, the hollow eyes and gaunt cheeks, the fear that was never far from the surface. They looked to him for hope, for answers, but what could he give them when he barely had hope himself? The weight of his responsibility was like a physical burden, pressing down on his chest, making it hard to breathe.

There were moments when the guilt became too much to bear. He would find himself alone, in the small confines of his office, staring at the photographs of the life he had once known—his family, his friends, all gone in the blink of an eye. He wondered what they would think of him now, if they would be proud of the man he had become, or if they would see him for what he feared he was: a man who was in over his head, trying to hold together the fragments of a broken world.

Karen, sensing his struggles, tried to offer support where she could. She would bring him reports of the day's progress, offer words of encouragement, and remind him that he wasn't alone in this fight. But even her reassurances couldn't banish the doubts that haunted him.

One evening, after a particularly grueling day of meetings and decisions, Karen found him in the command center, staring out into the darkness. The snow was falling heavily, the flakes swirling in the wind like ghosts. She approached him quietly, standing by his side as they both looked out at the frozen world beyond the glass.

"John," she said softly, "you're doing everything you can. We all are."

He didn't respond at first, his gaze fixed on the snow. Finally, he sighed, his breath fogging up the glass. "It's not enough, Karen. I can't shake the feeling that it's never going to be enough."

She turned to face him, her expression one of quiet determination. "You're carrying the weight of the world on your shoulders, John. But you don't have to do it alone. We're in this together, and we'll get through it together."

He looked at her then, seeing the exhaustion in her eyes, the same exhaustion he felt deep in his bones. But beneath it, there was a spark of hope, a determination that he envied. "I don't know if I can keep this up," he admitted, his voice barely above a whisper. "Every day, it feels like we're losing more ground. Like we're just delaying the inevitable."

Karen shook her head. "We're not delaying anything. We're fighting, John. And as long as we keep fighting, there's still hope. We owe it to everyone who didn't make it to keep going, to do whatever it takes to survive."

Her words struck a chord in him, reminding him of the promises he had made—not just to the people who looked to him for leadership, but to himself. He had vowed to rebuild, to restore, to recover. And as much as the weight of that vow bore down on him, he couldn't give up. Not when so many lives depended on him.

"We'll keep fighting," he agreed, his voice firmer now. "We'll do whatever it takes."

As they stood together, watching the snow fall, John felt a renewed sense of resolve. The road ahead was long, and the challenges were immense, but they couldn't afford to falter.

The harsh winter, the shortages, the guilt—they were all part of the burden he had to bear.

Chapter 7: The Fragmented States

The relentless winter continued to batter the base, its icy fingers clawing at the walls and windows. Inside, the air was filled with a tense silence as the gravity of their situation settled in. John sat at his desk, the faint light of a single lamp casting long shadows across the room. The maps and reports scattered before him were a stark reminder of the fractured state of the nation.

The realization had come slowly, as pieces of information from various regions began to coalesce. The United States, once a beacon of unity, was now a mosaic of isolated regions, each grappling with its own challenges. The federal government's attempts to maintain control had faltered, and what remained of the country was a fractured collection of territories, each struggling to survive.

Karen entered the office, her face lined with worry. She carried a stack of reports, the weight of their contents evident in her demeanor. "John, we've got more updates from the field," she said. "It's worse than we thought."

John looked up from the map he'd been studying, his eyes weary but determined. "How bad is it?"

Karen dropped the reports on the desk and began pointing out various regions on the map. "The United States has effectively fractured. We're seeing more and more evidence of rogue factions and local power struggles. The Pacific Alliance on the West Coast, the Southern Republic in the South—these groups have seized control of their respective areas and declared themselves independent."

John's heart sank as he took in the extent of the disintegration. The once-unified country was now a patchwork of rival factions, each with its own agenda and vision for the future. The chaos was not just a matter of logistical difficulties but a profound fracture in the very fabric of their society.

"Have we heard from any other regions?" John asked, his voice heavy with concern.

Karen started flipping through the reports. "We've received sporadic communications from some state leaders and military outposts. Many are trying to hold their ground, but they're often isolated and facing severe shortages. The smaller rogue groups are causing havoc, taking advantage of the breakdown in order."

John's mind raced with the implications. The challenges were not just about surviving the winter or managing scarce resources anymore; they were about reasserting authority over a nation that had slipped into anarchy. The federal government, already weakened, faced the additional challenge of dealing with these rogue factions that saw themselves as the new power centers.

"We need to re-establish some form of federal authority," John said, his voice resolute despite the exhaustion that dripped from his words. "We can't let these factions operate unchecked. We need to start by reaching out to these regional leaders, making it clear that we still represent the government, and that unity is essential for survival."

Karen's expression was a mixture of hope and skepticism. "Some of these leaders might be receptive. They might still see the value in a unified nation, even if it's just for practical reasons. But others…they've already declared themselves independent and might see any attempt at negotiation as a threat."

Acknowledging the truth in her words, John said, "We have to try. We need to present ourselves as a viable option for cooperation, not just an authority trying to impose control. If we can find common ground, we might be able to bring at least some of these factions back into the fold."

He turned his attention to General Moore, who had been reviewing the security situation. "General, I need you to coordinate efforts for outreach. We'll need to send envoys to the major factions, negotiate with their leaders, and attempt to re-establish some semblance of federal authority."

Moore's face now settled with an unsure look. "I'll start preparing the teams but we'll need to be cautious. These factions are heavily armed and have their own agendas. But if we can make contact and offer assistance, however we might just be able to sway some of them to our side."

The plan was set in motion quickly. Envoys were chosen—trusted individuals who had the skills and temperament to handle delicate negotiations. They would be tasked with reaching out to the leaders of the major factions, presenting the case for reunification, and offering aid in exchange for cooperation.

As the teams prepared to depart, John took a moment to reflect on the enormity of their mission. The nation was in disarray, and every faction they approached would be a potential battleground, each with its own set of demands and expectations. The road to re-establishing federal authority was fraught with challenges, and there was no guarantee of success.

John's own struggles were compounded by the weight of the responsibility he bore. The guilt of the past weeks, the unfulfilled promises, and the stark reality of leading a fractured nation all weighed heavily on him. He knew that the task ahead was monumental, and there were no easy answers.

As he walked through the base, observing the preparations and the worried faces of those who had come to rely on him, John felt the crushing burden of his role. The winter had been harsh, and the struggles they faced seemed unending. But there was a flicker of hope—a belief that despite the chaos, there was still a chance to rebuild.

The envoy teams set out into the frozen wasteland, carrying with them the hope of a nation struggling to find its way back from the brink of collapse. The journey would be fraught with danger and uncertainty, but it was a necessary step toward reuniting a shattered country.

In the quiet of the command center, John stood before the map once more, tracing the lines that marked the new boundaries of the fractured United States. The challenge ahead was immense, but he was determined to face it head-on. The future of the nation depended on their ability to overcome these divisions, to negotiate, and to find a way forward.

As the snow continued to fall outside, blanketing the world in a silent, cold embrace, John resolved to fight for the unity of his country. The road ahead would be long and fraught with challenges, but as long as there was a chance, he would do everything in his power to reunite the fractured union and guide it toward a future of hope and resilience.

Chapter 8: Reclaiming the Capitol

The winter had settled in deep, its cold grip unrelenting as the envoy teams departed for their missions. Inside the base, John and his remaining staff turned their focus restoring the symbol of American unity, Washington, D.C. The capital, long a symbol of the nation's strength and unity, had become a distant dream amidst the chaos. Rebuilding it was not just a matter of logistics but a powerful symbol of their resolve to restore the country's identity and governance.

The decision to restore Washington, D.C. was more than strategic—it was deeply symbolic. The city represented the heart of the federal government and re-establishing it as the capital was a powerful statement of their commitment to reuniting the fractured nation. But the task was monumental, fraught with physical and logistical challenges that seemed almost insurmountable.

John and his team gathered in the command center, where a large blueprint of Washington, D.C. covered a central table. The city, once a symbol of power and democracy, was now a shadow of its former self. Reports indicated that much of it had been destroyed or severely damaged by the nuclear fallout and subsequent turmoil.

Karen and General Moore joined John at the table, their faces etched with the strain of their recent efforts. Karen looked at the map with a sense of uneasy determination. "Restoring Washington, D.C. is going to be a huge undertaking. The city was heavily damaged, and radiation levels are still high in many areas. We'll need to address the immediate safety concerns before we can even begin reconstruction."

John acknowledged the enormity of the task. "We have to start somewhere. If we can establish a functioning government headquarters, it will be a significant step toward restoring order and demonstrating our commitment to rebuilding."

The initial plans focused on securing a small section of the city where the radiation levels were somewhat manageable.

The goal was to create a temporary government headquarters that could serve as a command center for coordinating the reconstruction efforts and re-establishing federal authority. It was a daunting task, but it was a necessary step in their broader mission.

General Moore was already working on mobilizing engineering teams and resources for the reconstruction. "We'll need to clear the debris, assess the structural integrity of any surviving buildings, and ensure that the area is safe for people to work in," he said, his voice steady despite the enormity of the challenge. "We'll also need to secure the perimeter to protect against any potential threats from the rogue factions or other dangers in the area."

John reviewed the logistics of the operation with his team. They would need to prioritize key infrastructure—communications, transportation routes, and basic utilities. The initial focus would be on creating a safe zone where essential operations could be conducted. This included setting up temporary living quarters for the construction teams, as well as a command center from which they could manage the rebuilding process.

As the plans took shape, the reality of the physical challenges became apparent. The city was not only physically devastated but also fraught with hidden dangers. Buildings had collapsed, streets were choked with debris, and the fallout had contaminated many areas. The teams would need to work carefully to avoid further exposure and ensure the safety of everyone involved.

The logistical challenges were equally daunting. The remnants of the transportation and supply networks were in disarray, making it difficult to transport materials and personnel to the site. The administration would have to rely on makeshift solutions, using whatever resources were available to piece together a functioning infrastructure.

Despite these challenges, there was a sense of purpose that drove the team forward. The symbolic importance of Washington, D.C. as the center of federal authority and unity made every obstacle worth overcoming. Rebuilding the capital would not only help re-establish governance but also serve as a beacon of hope for a nation desperately in need of direction.

The initial efforts were focused on setting up the temporary headquarters. The team selected a central location, an area that had suffered less damage than others and was somewhat shielded from the most severe radiation. The site would serve as the operational hub for coordinating the restoration of the city and, eventually, the re-establishment of the federal government.

John visited the site frequently, observing the progress and addressing any issues that arose. The sight of the construction teams working amidst the rubble, their efforts driven by a shared vision of renewal, filled him with a sense of cautious optimism. The work was slow and arduous, but each small step forward was a victory in and of itself.

As the temporary headquarters began to take shape, John and his team worked tirelessly to plan the next phases of reconstruction. The goal was not just to restore the physical infrastructure but also to send a powerful message of resilience and unity. The capital, once a symbol of the nation's strength, would become a symbol of its rebirth.

John knew that there was still a long road ahead. The challenges of re-establishing federal authority, dealing with rogue factions, and managing the widespread devastation would test their resolve at every turn. But the act of rebuilding Washington, D.C. was a critical step in reuniting the nation and restoring its sense of identity and purpose.

As winter gave way to the first signs of spring, the temporary headquarters stood as a testament to their determination. The work was far from over, but the progress made was a sign that hope was not lost.

Chapter 9: The Council of Reconciliation

While the temporary headquarters in Washington, D.C. began to stabilize, John and his team recognized the urgent need to address the fragmentation of the country. With the symbolic importance of restoring the capital and the physical challenges of reconstruction on their plate, the next crucial step was to convene a council that would bring together the governors of surviving states and the leaders of independent regions.

The conference room was meticulously prepared for this meeting. The large table was covered with maps, satellite images, and an array of documents detailing the current state of various regions. A sense of gravity hung in the air as representatives from across the fractured nation took their seats, each bringing with them the weight of their region's struggles and aspirations.

John stood at the head of the table, flanked by Karen and General Moore. His voice carried a blend of resolve and empathy as he addressed the room. "Thank you all for coming to this critical meeting. The state of our nation demands that we come together to address our immediate needs and to discuss how we can rebuild and reunite."

The leaders, a diverse group with varied backgrounds and perspectives, listened intently. Among them were Governor Lyla Martin of the Pacific Alliance, a determined woman who had managed to rally her region despite severe resource shortages; Governor Richard Fields of the Southern Republic, a former military leader with a strong grip on his territory; and several independent faction leaders who had carved out their own domains in the wake of the chaos.

John began by outlining the agenda for the meeting: addressing immediate needs, discussing resource distribution, and tackling the issue of authority and governance. The council's first task was to assess and address the immediate needs of the country—food, water, medical supplies, and shelter.

Governor Lyla Martin was the first to speak. Her face was lined with exhaustion, but her voice was steady. "In the Pacific Alliance, we're facing dire shortages of essential supplies. Our agricultural base was devastated, and we've had trouble securing clean water. The situation is critical, and we need more support from the federal government to ensure our people can survive the winter."

Governor Fields nodded in agreement, though his expression was more guarded. "The Southern Republic has managed to maintain some stability, but we're also experiencing shortages. We've been able to manage with what we have, but the pressure is mounting. We need to ensure that resources are distributed in a way that's fair and effective."

The discussion quickly heated up as each leader presented their case. The room was filled with competing voices, each arguing for the needs of their respective regions. The central issue was how to fairly allocate the limited resources available, given the varied needs and conditions across the country.

John and his team listened carefully, taking notes and considering the implications of each argument. The debate highlighted the deep divisions that remained, but it also underscored the urgent need for a coordinated response. Karen intervened, proposing a solution. "We need to establish a temporary framework for resource distribution. This framework should prioritize the most critical needs and ensure that resources are allocated based on severity and urgency."

The council agreed to form a subcommittee to develop this framework. The subcommittee would be responsible for creating a system for assessing needs and distributing resources in a way that aimed to be equitable and effective. This was a step toward addressing the immediate crisis and setting a precedent for future cooperation.

The next major topic of discussion was the balance of authority between the federal government and the regional leaders. The independent faction leaders were particularly concerned about the extent of federal control and how it might impact their independence. The debate was intense, with varying views on how much authority should be centralized versus decentralized.

General Moore proposed a balanced approach. "We need to create a governance structure that respects the autonomy of each region while allowing for effective federal oversight. This could involve establishing a council with representatives from both the federal government and regional leaders to oversee key decisions and ensure that the needs of all regions are considered."

The proposal was met with a mix of approval and skepticism. Some leaders were receptive, seeing it as a way to maintain their autonomy while still participating in a unified governance structure. Others were wary, concerned about the potential for federal overreach.

As the debates continued, John made a strategic decision to focus on building trust among the leaders. He emphasized the importance of collaboration and mutual respect. "Our goal is to create a system that works for everyone. We need to recognize that while our regions have unique needs and perspectives, we all share a common goal—rebuilding our nation and ensuring its survival."

To facilitate this process, John proposed that this headquarters would serve as the operational center for coordinating the recovery efforts and managing the transition to a more permanent governance structure. The idea was to create a neutral ground where leaders could meet, discuss, and make decisions in a collaborative environment. The council agreed to move forward with this plan.

As the meeting drew to a close, there was a sense of cautious optimism. The council had made some progress in addressing the immediate needs of the country and had taken the first steps toward establishing a framework for governance. The road ahead was still fraught with challenges, but the fact that leaders from across the country were coming together to negotiate and collaborate was a promising sign.

John looked out over the assembled leaders, feeling a mixture of hope and resolve. "Thank you all for your contributions today. We've made important strides, but there is much more work ahead. Let's continue to approach this process with the spirit of cooperation and dedication to the greater good. Together, we can rebuild our nation and move toward a future of unity and resilience."

As the leaders departed, the atmosphere was charged with a renewed sense of purpose. The council had laid the groundwork for reuniting the nation, and while the journey was far from over, the steps taken today represented a critical turning point. The process of healing and reconstruction had begun in earnest, and the promise of a united future was within reach.

Chapter 10: The Scavenger Missions

While the newly established council continued its work, one of the most pressing challenges was addressing the severe shortages of essential supplies and technology. The temporary government headquarters had begun to function, but the nation's ability to rebuild depended heavily on recovering crucial resources from areas devastated by the nuclear fallout.

John recognized the gravity of the situation. The infrastructure required to support the recovery effort—power plants, communication systems, and medical facilities—was in disrepair. The supply lines were fragile, and many critical resources were located in hazardous areas or had been lost in the chaos of the disaster. To address these issues, organized expeditions were necessary.

In the command center, John gathered his team to discuss the plans for these expeditions. The room was filled with maps, logistical reports, and lists of needed supplies. Karen and General Moore were by his side, both deeply involved in planning the missions.

"Our first priority is to recover essential supplies and technology," John said, pointing to a map of the surrounding regions. "We need to identify the locations of critical resources and organize expeditions to retrieve them. The risks are significant, but these resources are vital for rebuilding our infrastructure."

Karen nodded her head in agreement. "We've identified several key locations where we believe important supplies and technology are stored. These include power plants, communications hubs, and medical stockpiles. However, many of these areas are still heavily contaminated or occupied by hostile groups."

General Moore added, "We'll need to carefully plan our routes and ensure that each team is well-equipped to handle the dangers they might encounter. Radiation zones and potential threats from rogue factions will be significant challenges."

John took a deep breath, understanding the gravity of the situation. "We'll need to establish a few key teams for these expeditions. Each team should have a clear objective, specialized equipment for radiation protection, and enough resources to complete their mission. I want to be involved in the planning and oversight of these missions to ensure that everything goes smoothly."

The planning sessions that followed were intense and detailed. The teams were organized based on their objectives, and each was assigned specific tasks. Some teams were to recover technology and communications equipment from damaged government buildings and tech facilities. Others were tasked with retrieving medical supplies from hospitals and research centers.

One of the most critical expeditions was to a nearby power plant that had been abandoned but was essential for restoring electrical power to the temporary headquarters and surrounding areas. The plant was located in a highly contaminated zone, and the team assigned to this mission would need to navigate through dangerous terrain and radiation levels.

John personally reviewed the plans for this mission. "The power plant recovery is a high-priority mission. We need to restore power as soon as possible to support our operations and provide for the needs of the people. The team will be equipped with advanced radiation suits and Geiger counters. We'll also have a team of engineers on standby to help with any technical issues once the site is secured."

As the expeditions began, John remained actively involved, coordinating with the teams, reviewing progress reports, and addressing any issues that arose. The missions were fraught with danger. The radiation zones were a constant threat, and the risk of hostile encounters with rogue factions or scavengers was ever-present.

One of the expeditions, led by Lieutenant Sarah Collins, encountered severe challenges. As her team approached a former tech facility, they found the area heavily irradiated and occupied by a group of hostile scavengers. The team had to use both their radiation gear and tactical skills to secure the site and retrieve the necessary equipment. John was in constant communication with Sarah, providing support and making decisions as the situation evolved.

Despite these difficulties, the expeditions were largely successful. The teams managed to recover essential supplies, including crucial technology and medical equipment. The power plant team restored electricity to the temporary headquarters, which was a significant milestone in the recovery effort. The communications equipment retrieved from the tech facility allowed for better coordination and improved communication between the different regions.

John's involvement in the planning and oversight of these missions proved invaluable. His hands-on approach helped ensure that the expeditions were well-coordinated and that any problems were addressed promptly. The successful recovery of resources was a major boost to the rebuilding efforts and provided a much-needed morale lift.

As the expeditions continued, the temporary headquarters became increasingly operational. The recovered supplies were used to repair infrastructure, restore services, and support the ongoing efforts to reunite and rebuild the nation. Each success in the field translated into tangible improvements in the quality of life for the survivors and strengthened the foundation for future recovery.

John stood in the command center, reviewing the latest reports with Karen and General Moore. The progress was encouraging, but there was still much work to be done. "We've made significant strides, but we need to remain vigilant. The challenges are far from over, and we must continue to push forward with determination and caution."

Karen replied. "The expeditions have been crucial in restoring our capabilities. The next phase will involve integrating these resources into our broader recovery plan and addressing the ongoing needs of the population."

Chapter 11: The New Constitution

The temporary headquarters of the federal government, housed in what had once been a grand hotel, was abuzz with activity. In the war-torn remnants of what used to be the capital, the seeds of a new nation were about to be sown. The nuclear war had shattered not just cities but the very fabric of the United States. The Constitution, once a beacon of democracy and rule of law, now felt like a relic of a world that no longer existed.

The President had long known this moment would come. Since the first bombs fell, the country had been drifting, held together only by the thinnest threads of loyalty, fear, and necessity. But those threads were fraying. The United States was splintering, with regions and factions carving out their own territories, driven by the desperation to survive. The old ways of governance, the old rules, no longer applied.

John stood in a conference room that had been hastily converted into a meeting space, surrounded by maps, charts, and stacks of intelligence reports. The once-grand room, with its crystal chandeliers and faded murals, now bore the scars of war—cracked walls, shattered windows boarded up with sheets of metal, and a thick layer of dust that seemed impossible to completely remove. It was here that the future of the country would be decided.

Karen, stood beside him, reviewing a list of the delegates who would be arriving over the next few days. "We've confirmed attendance from all the major regions," she said, her voice filled with both anticipation and caution. "The Pacific Alliance, the Southern Republic, and even a new territory called the Mountain States have agreed to send representatives, though they're still skeptical."

John's face was etched with the strain of leadership. "Skeptical or not, we need them here. If we're going to forge a new path forward, it has to be together. This isn't just about survival anymore—it's about building something that can last."

The task ahead was monumental. The old Constitution, revered as it was, had been crafted for a nation of abundance, of peace, of relative stability. The post-apocalyptic United States was none of those things. It was a country on the brink of collapse, where survival often outweighed ideology, and where the central government's authority was more theoretical than practical. A new framework was needed—one that could address the immediate challenges of survival while laying the groundwork for a more stable and just future.

The constitutional convention was set to begin in just a few days. It was to be the most important gathering in American history since the original Constitutional Convention of 1787. But this time, the stakes were even higher. Failure would mean not just the end of the United States as a unified nation, but the descent into chaos and endless warlords battling for control of the remnants.

As the delegates began to arrive, the atmosphere in the temporary headquarters became electric with tension. Governors, military leaders, representatives from the independent regions, and experts from various fields all gathered, each bringing with them the weight of their own region's survival and their own vision for what the future should look like. Many of them had never met before, and some had been on opposing sides of the conflicts that had erupted in the wake of the bombings.

The first day of the convention was marked by a palpable sense of unease. The delegates assembled in the grand ballroom, a space that had once hosted lavish events, now stark and utilitarian with rows of tables and chairs set up under the dim light of emergency lamps. The air was thick with the smell of smoke and ash, a constant reminder of the destruction outside.

John opened the convention with a speech that acknowledged the gravity of the situation. He spoke not just as the President, but as a fellow survivor, a leader who had lost as much as anyone else. "We stand at a crossroads," he began, his voice firm but carrying the weight of emotion. "The world as we knew it is gone. But we are still here. And as long as we are here, we have a duty to those who did not survive, to those who will come after us, and to ourselves, to build something better from the ashes."

He paused, looking around the room at the faces of the delegates—hardened by war, by loss, but also by determination. "This convention is not just about creating a new government. It's about ensuring that the principles of freedom, justice, and equality, which have always defined us as a nation, are not lost. But we must also be realistic. The world has changed, and we must change with it."

The days that followed were a whirlwind of debate and discussion. The first major topic was how to govern a post-apocalyptic United States. The old federal system, with its checks and balances, seemed inadequate to deal with the immediate challenges of survival—scarcity of resources, security threats, and the need for rapid decision-making. Yet, there was also a deep fear of concentrating too much power in any one branch of government, particularly in a world where the old norms and safeguards had been eroded.

Delegates from the Pacific Alliance, a region that had managed to maintain a semblance of order and prosperity through a strong, centralized government, argued for a similar model at the national level. "We need a government that can act decisively," their representative stated, his voice carrying across the room. "In times like these, too much debate can be paralyzing. We need strong leadership, and we need it now."

But others, particularly those from the more fragmented regions, where local leaders had taken control, were wary of such a model. "We've seen what happens when power is concentrated in the hands of a few," said a representative from the Mountain States, his tone measured but firm. "In our region, we've survived because we've adapted—by giving more autonomy to local communities. People need to have a say in their own survival. We can't afford to impose a one-size-fits-all solution."

John listened carefully to both sides, understanding that this was the crux of the challenge—finding a balance between the need for strong, effective governance and the need to preserve the rights and autonomy of the regions. He knew that whatever solution they came up with, it would have to be flexible enough to accommodate the diverse needs and realities of the different parts of the country.

One proposal that gained traction was the idea of a hybrid system—one that allowed for strong regional governments but also maintained a central authority for matters of national importance, such as defense, trade, and the management of resources. This system would be different from the old federal model, with more clearly defined powers for the regions, but with a central government that had the ability to act decisively in times of crisis.

As the debate over governance continued, another critical issue arose: the need for a new Constitution that would reflect the realities of this changed world. The delegates quickly realized that this was not just a legal document they were drafting—it was a manifesto for the future of the country, a blueprint that would determine how they would live, govern, and interact with one another in this new era.

The proposal for a new Constitution sparked intense debate. Some delegates argued that the existing Constitution, with some amendments, could still serve as the foundation for the new government. Others, however, believed that the changes needed were so profound that a completely new document was necessary.

John understood both perspectives. The old Constitution had been the bedrock of American democracy, but it had been created for a world that no longer existed. He knew that whatever they decided, it had to be something that all the regions could agree on, something that would give them hope and a sense of shared purpose.

As the convention continued, John took on the role of a mediator, guiding the discussions with a careful hand. He knew that his job was not to impose his own views, but to help the delegates find common ground. It was a delicate balancing act, requiring both patience and decisiveness.

One of the most heated debates centered around the issue of emergency powers. In the aftermath of the nuclear war, the government had been forced to take drastic measures to maintain order—rationing of resources, curfews, and martial law in some areas. These measures had been necessary, but they had also raised concerns about the erosion of civil liberties.

The question now was how to balance the need for security with the preservation of individual rights. Some delegates argued for strong emergency powers that could be invoked in times of crisis, while others feared that such powers could be abused.

John weighed in on this debate with a proposal that struck a middle ground. He suggested that the new Constitution include provisions for emergency powers, but with strict limits and oversight. "We must be able to respond swiftly to crises," he said, "but we must also ensure that these powers are not used as a tool of oppression. There should be clear checks and balances, and these powers should be temporary, with regular review by both the executive and legislative branches."

This proposal was met with cautious approval. It addressed the immediate need for strong governance while also preserving the principles of accountability and the rule of law. It was a compromise, but one that many felt was necessary in the new world they were living in.

Another significant challenge was the question of how to protect individual rights in a world where resources were scarce, and survival often took precedence over ideology. The original Bill of Rights had enshrined freedoms that were now under threat—freedom of speech, the right to bear arms, protection against unreasonable searches and seizures. But in the chaos of the post-apocalyptic world, these rights had been compromised.

The delegates debated fiercely over this issue. Some argued that in times of crisis, certain rights might need to be curtailed to ensure the survival of the community. Others insisted that these rights were non-negotiable, that they were the very essence of what it meant to be American.

John understood the passion on both sides. He knew that the preservation of civil liberties was crucial to maintaining the moral foundation of the country, but he also recognized the harsh realities they faced. He proposed that the new Constitution reaffirm the rights enshrined in the original Bill of Rights, but with provisions that allowed for temporary, narrowly defined restrictions in times of extreme crisis, subject to judicial review.

This was another difficult compromise, but it was one that most of the delegates could agree on. It provided a framework for protecting individual rights while also acknowledging the need for flexibility in times of crisis.

As the convention neared an end, the delegates turned their attention to the structure of the government itself. There was broad agreement that the new government needed to be more adaptable and responsive than the old system, but there was less consensus on the specifics.

Some delegates pushed for a more decentralized system, where regions had greater control over their own affairs. They argued that the diversity of the post-apocalyptic United States required a system that could accommodate different needs and realities. Others, however, feared that too much decentralization could lead to fragmentation and weaken the ability of the government to respond to national crises.

After days of intense discussion, the convention settled on a hybrid model. The new government would have a strong central authority, particularly in areas like defense, trade, and resource management, but it would also give significant autonomy to the regions. This would allow for flexibility and adaptability while maintaining a unified national framework.

The final days of the convention were spent refining the details of the new Constitution. It was a massive undertaking, with delegates working late into the night to draft and revise the document. Every word was carefully considered, every clause debated and scrutinized. It was a labor of love, but also of necessity—this document would be the foundation of the new United States, and it had to be right.

Finally, after weeks of intense work, the new Constitution was completed. It was a document that reflected the harsh realities of the new world but also the enduring values of the old. It provided for a government that could respond to crises with strength and decisiveness, but also one that protected the rights and freedoms of its citizens.

The signing ceremony was a momentous occasion. The delegates gathered in the grand ballroom, now transformed into a solemn and historic space. The air was thick with anticipation as each delegate stepped forward to sign the new Constitution. There was a sense of both accomplishment and gravity—everyone present knew that they were making history.

John was the last to sign. As he approached the table, he felt the weight of the moment. This was more than just a document—it was a promise to the future, a commitment to rebuilding a nation that had been nearly destroyed. With a steady hand, he signed his name, sealing the work that they had all done.

In his final address to the delegates, John spoke of the road ahead. "What we have done here today is nothing short of extraordinary," he said, his voice filled with emotion. "We have taken the first steps toward rebuilding our country, not just in terms of infrastructure, but in terms of what we stand for as a people. This new Constitution is a symbol of our resilience and our commitment to a better future. It won't be easy, but together, we can and will overcome the challenges ahead."

As the delegates began to disperse, returning to their regions to implement the new government, John stood alone in the ballroom for a moment, taking it all in. The future was still uncertain, and there were many challenges ahead, but for the first time in a long while, he felt a sense of hope. The new Constitution was a beacon in the darkness, a guide for the difficult journey ahead. And with it, he believed, they could rebuild not just the United States, but a better, stronger nation for the future.

Chapter 12: Family Comes First

The air in the command vehicle was thick with tension, every breath John took seeming to catch in his throat. The hum of the tires on the cracked road was the only sound that punctuated the oppressive silence inside. Outside, the world was a shattered, desolate place, the remnants of a once-thriving nation now lying in ruins. The convoy cut through the night like a spear, its headlights slicing through the darkness, but the deeper they went, the more John felt a growing sense of dread gnawing at him.

General Moore, seated beside him, had just delivered the news that had sent a shockwave through John's entire being. The bunker where his family had been sent to safety had been located. For months, they had searched relentlessly, following every lead, every rumor, clinging to the fragile hope that his wife and children were alive, waiting for him to find them. Now, they were so close—just a few more miles—and the anticipation was almost unbearable.

"Sir, we're approaching the site," Moore said, his voice low, filled with the weight of the situation.

John wanted to reply but his throat was too tight to respond. His mind raced with thoughts of his family—of his wife's gentle smile, his children's laughter. He had imagined this moment countless times, the joyous reunion, the tears of relief, the sense of wholeness that had been missing for so long. But as the convoy neared the bunker, a cold chill settled over him. The bunker should have been a place of safety, but something felt wrong—terribly, horribly wrong.

The convoy slowed as they reached their destination. John leaned forward, peering out the window, and his heart sank. The entrance to the bunker was barely recognizable, half-buried under rubble and overgrown with weeds. The massive steel doors, designed to withstand the deadliest of attacks, were ajar, twisted and scarred as if something monstrous had clawed its way inside.

"Hold the perimeter!" Moore barked to the soldiers, who immediately fanned out, weapons at the ready. The air was heavy with the smell of decay and burnt metal, a nauseating combination that made John's stomach turn. He forced himself out of the vehicle, his legs unsteady beneath him. Every instinct screamed at him to run inside, to find his family, but Moore's firm hand on his arm held him back.

"Mr. President, let us secure the area first," Moore said, his tone leaving no room for argument.

John clenched his fists, every fiber of his being resisting the urge to charge forward. He nodded, knowing Moore was right, but the waiting was torture. He stood there, his eyes locked on the gaping maw of the bunker entrance, each second stretching into an eternity. The silence was deafening, broken only by the distant sounds of the soldiers moving into position.

Finally, Moore signaled to a group of soldiers, and they moved into the bunker, their figures swallowed by the darkness within. John's heart pounded in his chest, each beat a thunderous roar in his ears. He strained to hear something—anything—that would give him a clue as to what lay inside. But the minutes dragged on, and with each passing moment, his fear grew, coiling tighter around his chest like a vise.

Then came the first sign—one of the soldiers emerged, his face pale, eyes wide with something akin to horror. He quickly averted his gaze from John, and in that moment, John knew. The hope that had sustained him for so long began to crack, splintering under the weight of what was to come.

A few agonizing minutes later, Moore himself reappeared, his usually stern face now etched with grief. He walked slowly towards John, each step heavy with the burden of what he was about to say. John's breath caught in his throat, his mind screaming in denial even as his body began to betray him, knees weakening, vision blurring.

"Mr. President…" Moore's voice was thick with emotion, his eyes brimming with sorrow. "I'm so sorry… they didn't make it."

The words crashed over John like a tidal wave, sweeping away the last remnants of his composure. His legs buckled, and he collapsed to the ground, the world spinning around him. The grief was immediate and all-consuming, a raw, searing pain that tore through him with unrelenting force.

He gasped for air, his chest heaving, but the weight of the loss was crushing, suffocating.

"No… no, no, no…" The words spilled from him in a broken whisper, his voice cracking under the strain. He pounded the ground with his fists, as if the physical pain could somehow drown out the agony in his heart. "Not them… please, not them…"

Moore knelt beside him, his hand resting on John's shoulder, offering what little comfort he could. The soldiers stood at a respectful distance, their heads bowed, sharing in the President's grief. They had seen the horrors inside the bunker—the signs of a desperate struggle, the destruction left in the wake of those who had raided it. They had seen the lifeless bodies of John's wife and children, hidden away in the depths of what was supposed to be their sanctuary.

The idea that his family had died in such a place, alone and terrified, was a wound too deep to bear. John's sobs echoed through the desolate landscape, a haunting sound that seemed to reverberate off the ruins around them. He had led a nation through its darkest days, but this… this was a pain he had not been prepared for, a loss that threatened to consume him whole.

For what felt like an eternity, John remained on the ground, lost in his grief, the world around him fading to nothing. The man who had held the nation together, who had borne the weight of leadership through unimaginable trials, was now a broken shell, crushed under the enormity of his personal tragedy.

But even in the depths of his despair, a small, stubborn spark refused to die. Somewhere deep inside, he knew that he could not give in, that he had to find the strength to go on—not just for himself, but for the memory of his family, and for the millions of survivors who still depended on him. The future of the nation was still in his hands, and he could not abandon them, no matter how much he wanted to.

With a great effort, John forced himself to his feet, his body trembling with the strain. He wiped the tears from his eyes, though the pain still lingered, a dull ache that would never fully go away. Moore was there, steady and resolute, ready to support him in whatever came next.

"We need to move," John said, his voice hoarse but filled with a renewed sense of purpose. "There's still work to be done."

Moore agreed, understanding the resolve in John's words. The convoy would continue, the mission would go on, because it had to. But as they left the bunker behind, John knew that a part of him would remain there forever, buried with the family he had loved and lost.

The road ahead was dark and fraught with challenges, but John was determined to see it through. He had lost everything, but in the process, he had found a new reason to fight—a reason to rebuild, to create a future that his family would have been proud of. And so, with a heavy heart but an unbroken spirit, John pressed on, determined to lead his nation out of the darkness and into the light of a new dawn.

Chapter 13: The Rebellion

A couple weeks later John found himself standing in the command room that was filled with a low hum of anxious voices and the persistent tapping of keyboards as reports flowed in from across the fractured nation. John stood at the large window, staring out at the bleak, overcast sky. The weather mirrored his mood—gray, heavy, and filled with grief.

"Mr. President, we have a situation," General Moore's voice cut through the tension in the room. John turned to face him, bracing himself for more bad news.

"What is it, General?" John asked, his voice weary yet steady.

Moore stepped forward, his expression as dark as the reports he held. "A major rebellion has erupted in the Midwest. It's not just a skirmish; this is a coordinated effort. They've seized several key supply depots and communication hubs. If we don't act quickly, this could spiral out of control."

John's heart sank. The signs had been there—whispers of unrest, growing frustration among the population, the mounting distrust of the federal government—but he had hoped they could address the issues before they reached a boiling point. Now, it seemed, that hope was in vain.

"What are their demands?" John asked, trying to remain calm and focused.

Moore sighed heavily, handing over a report. "Autonomy, control over local resources, and the end of federal authority in their region. But it's more than just demands. The rebellion is fueled by fear, scarcity, and the belief that the government can't protect them anymore."

John scanned the report, his eyes narrowing at the details. The leaders of the rebellion were former state officials, military deserters, and local militia heads—people who had once sworn allegiance to the United States, now turning against it. The reasons were as varied as the individuals involved: some were motivated by survival, others by power, and many by sheer desperation.

"How did we get here, General?" John asked, more to himself than to Moore. "How did we go from a united front against a common enemy to this?"

Moore didn't have an answer. He simply shook his head. "Fear is a powerful weapon, Mr. President. And it's been used against us."

John's mind raced as he considered their options. The country was already on the brink, with food shortages, contaminated water supplies, and the ever-present threat of radiation. The harsh winter had only made things worse, straining resources and pushing people to the edge. Now, this rebellion threatened to tear apart what little remained of the nation.

"We need to quell this rebellion before it spreads," John said, his voice firm. "But we can't afford to ignite a civil war. We need to find a way to bring these people back to the table, to show them that we're still fighting for them, not against them."

Moore replied in agreement with the situation. "I've already dispatched scouts to gather intelligence on the rebel leaders.

We have a few contacts who might be willing to negotiate, but it's a gamble. They're angry, and they don't trust us."

John walked over to the map on the wall, his fingers tracing the regions that had fallen under rebel control. "We'll start by reaching out to those willing to talk," he said. "Offer them a chance to voice their concerns and propose solutions. But make it clear that violence will not be tolerated."

Moore began drafting the orders as John continued to study the map. His mind was a whirlwind of thoughts—strategies, potential alliances, the risks of escalation. Every decision he made now carried enormous weight, not just for the present, but for the future of the entire country.

As the night wore on, John found himself alone in his office, staring at the ceiling. The quiet was oppressive, filled with the echoes of his thoughts and fears. He could feel the burden of his position more acutely than ever before. The rebellion wasn't just a threat to the nation—it was a direct challenge to his leadership, a test of his ability to hold the country together in its darkest hour.

He thought of his family, the weight of their loss pressing down on him like a physical force. The pain was still raw, and the memory of their final moments haunted him. But he couldn't allow himself to be consumed by grief. The people still needed him, and he had to be strong, even when he felt like he was breaking inside.

The following morning, John addressed the nation in a radio broadcast, his voice calm but resolute. "My fellow Americans, we are facing unprecedented challenges. The scars of the war are deep, and the path to recovery is long. But we cannot afford to turn against each other. We must remember that our strength lies in our unity, in our shared belief in the future of this great nation. I urge those who have taken up arms to stand down, to come to the table and discuss your grievances. We will listen, and we will find a way forward together."

The message was clear: the government was willing to negotiate, but it would not tolerate rebellion. It was a delicate balance, one that would require all of John's diplomatic skills to maintain.

Days passed and the tension in the air only grew thicker. Reports came in from across the country—skirmishes between federal troops and rebel forces, raids on supply convoys, acts of sabotage against critical infrastructure. The rebellion was spreading, and the administration was stretched thin, struggling to keep control.

In the command room, John and Moore pored over maps and reports, trying to anticipate the rebels' next moves. "We need to cut off their supply lines," Moore said, tracing a route on the map. "If we can isolate them, we might be able to force a surrender."

"But we can't afford to cut off supplies to the civilian population," John countered. "We're already dealing with shortages. If we choke off supplies, we risk pushing more people into the rebels' arms."

Moore frowned, acknowledging the dilemma. "Then we need to find another way to disrupt their operations. We could target their communication networks, spread misinformation, sow discord among their ranks."

John considered this. It was a risky strategy, but it might buy them the time they needed to bring the rebels to the negotiating table. "Do it," he said. "But make sure we minimize civilian casualties. We can't lose any more support from the people."

As the military operation unfolded, John found himself increasingly isolated. The demands of leadership left little room for personal reflection, but the weight of his decisions pressed heavily on him. The rebellion had brought the administration to the brink, and the stakes had never been higher.

Amidst the chaos, John's thoughts often drifted to his family, to the life he had lost. He wondered if they would have been proud of him, if they would have understood the choices he had to make. The pain was always there, just beneath the surface, but he buried it deep, knowing he couldn't afford to show weakness.

One evening, as he sat in his office, John received word that one of the rebel leaders had agreed to meet. It was a small victory, but it gave him a glimmer of hope. The meeting was set for a neutral location, and John insisted on attending in person, despite the risks.

The meeting took place in the ruins of a courthouse, now a shell of its former self. The walls were cracked, the windows shattered, but it was a fitting symbol of the state of the nation—a reminder of what had been lost and what was still at stake.

John entered the courthouse, flanked by General Moore and a small contingent of soldiers. The rebel leader, a stern-looking man in his fifties, stood at the far end of the room, his eyes cold and calculating. He had once been a governor, a man of power and influence, but now he was a leader of a rebellion that threatened to tear the country apart.

"Mr. President," the rebel leader said, his voice laced with contempt. "I never thought I'd see the day when you'd come crawling to us."

John didn't rise to the bait. He had expected hostility, and he knew this man was testing him, trying to gauge his resolve. "I'm here to find a solution," John replied evenly. "We both know that this rebellion is tearing the country apart. We can either find a way to end it peacefully, or we can continue down this path and destroy everything we've worked to rebuild."

The rebel leader's eyes narrowed. "And what makes you think we're interested in peace? We're fighting for our survival, for our right to govern ourselves without interference from Washington."

John took a step closer, his gaze steady. "And what makes you think you'll survive without the support of the rest of the country? We're stronger together, and you know it. If we fall apart now, there won't be anything left to govern."

There was a long silence as the two men stared each other down. The tension in the room was palpable, each side waiting for the other to make a move.

Finally, the rebel leader spoke, his tone grudgingly respectful. "I'll consider your proposal, Mr. President. But make no mistake—if we don't see real change, this rebellion will continue, and it will spread."

John replied, knowing this was the best outcome he could hope for at the moment. "Then let's work together to make that change happen."

As the meeting ended, and John made his way back to the base, he couldn't shake the feeling that the battle was far from over. The rebellion had exposed the deep fractures within the country, and even if they managed to quell it, the underlying issues would remain.

Back at the base, John collapsed into his chair, the exhaustion overwhelming him. The day's events had taken a toll, and the weight of responsibility was heavier than ever. He closed his eyes, just for a moment, letting the weariness wash over him.

But sleep would not come. His mind was too full of worries—about the rebellion, about the future of the nation, about the countless lives that depended on his decisions. The pressure was relentless, and he felt it pressing down on him like a vice.

As the night wore on, John knew that the fight was far from over. The rebellion was just one of many challenges they would face in the days and weeks to come. But he also knew that he couldn't afford to give up. The country needed him, now more than ever.

The future was uncertain, the road ahead treacherous, but John was determined to see it through. He had to believe that there was still hope, that the nation could be rebuilt from the ashes. And as long as that hope remained, he would keep fighting, no matter the cost.

Chapter 14: The Legacy of War

The camp bustled with a quiet urgency as survivors moved about their tasks, a sense of needed determination uniting them. It was late afternoon, the sky a pale, cold blue, as President Anderson and Karen stood together in the heart of the encampment. The ground beneath them was hard, still frozen in places from the harsh winter that had followed the nuclear fallout. The air was heavy with the unspoken grief that hung over the camp—a grief that had become as much a part of their lives as the scarcity of food and the threat of rogue factions.

In front of them, a large open space had been cleared, marked with makeshift boundaries of stones and wood. This would be the site of the first national memorial—a place where survivors could come to remember those they had lost in the war. The decision to create this memorial had come after many days of discussion, as John and his administration grappled with how to address the psychological and cultural devastation wrought by the nuclear conflict.

The ground was bare now, a blank canvas waiting to be filled with memories and sorrow. John gazed out over the space, imagining what it would look like in the future—rows of stones, engraved with names and messages, surrounded by simple sculptures and plaques that would tell the story of a nation brought to its knees, and of the resilience that had allowed it to rise again.

"We need to give people a way to process what's happened," Karen said softly, breaking the silence. Her voice carried the weight of her own losses, yet there was a quiet strength in it that John had come to rely on. "This memorial isn't just about honoring the dead. It's about helping the living find a way to move forward."

John replied with his thoughts heavy. "We've lost so much, Karen. Families, communities, entire cities… How do we even begin to heal from something like this?"

Karen's eyes reflected the same sorrow John felt, but also a fierce determination. "We start here. We start by acknowledging the pain, by giving people a place to grieve and to remember. And from that grief, we build something new—something that honors the past but also gives us hope for the future."

John took a deep breath, letting Karen's words sink in. She was right, of course. The survivors needed more than just food and shelter; they needed a way to make sense of the senseless, to find meaning in a world that had been stripped of so much.

Together, they walked the perimeter of the memorial site, discussing how it would be organized. They envisioned a central monument—a tall, unadorned obelisk of stone, to symbolize the strength and endurance of the human spirit. Around it would be smaller markers, each one representing a life lost, a family destroyed, a community obliterated. Survivors would be encouraged to bring personal items to leave at the site—photographs, letters, mementos of loved ones—creating a living testament to those who had been taken.

"We'll need to establish guidelines," John said, his mind already racing with logistical considerations. "We'll need materials, volunteers to help with the construction, and a way to record and organize the names. And we need to make sure this isn't just a one-time effort. Every settlement should have a place like this."

Karen responded in agreement. "We should also involve the survivors in the process. Let them take ownership of it. It'll be a way for them to connect with each other, to share their stories. It could help them rebuild a sense of community."

They paused at the center of the site, where the central monument would stand. The cold wind swept through the camp, carrying with it the faint sounds of hammering and sawing as the survivors worked to rebuild their lives. John glanced at Karen, who was staring at the empty space with a distant look in her eyes.

"You haven't said much about your family," John said gently, sensing that something was weighing on her.

Karen's gaze remained fixed on the ground for a moment before she finally spoke. "I found out yesterday that my mother didn't make it. She was in one of the cities that was hit."

John's heart clenched at her words. He knew all too well the pain that came with losing family to the war. "Karen... I'm so sorry."

Karen shook her head, blinking back tears. "She was everything to me, John. She raised me on her own. She was the reason I got into politics—to make her proud, to make a difference. And now she's gone, just like so many others."

John placed a hand on her shoulder, offering what comfort he could. "I know what it's like. I lost my family too. My wife, my children... They were my world. And now... now all I have left is this."

He gestured to the camp around them, the survivors moving like shadows through the gathering dusk. "We've both lost so much, Karen. But we have to keep going. We have to make sure their deaths weren't in vain."

Karen turned to him, her expression fierce despite the tears that glistened in her eyes. "We will, John. We'll build something better, something that honors their memory. We owe it to them, and to everyone who's still here, to keep fighting."

Together, they stood in the growing darkness, united by their shared grief and their shared resolve. The camp around them was a testament to the resilience of the human spirit, but it was also a reminder of the long road ahead—a road that would be marked by pain, by loss, but also by hope.

As the first stars began to appear in the night sky, John made a silent vow. They would build this memorial, and others like it, across the country. They would honor the past, but they would also build a future where such a tragedy would never happen again. And through it all, they would remember those who had been lost, and carry their memories forward into the new world they were creating.

"We should get started on this," John said quietly, breaking the silence. "We'll need to gather the survivors, explain what we're doing. And then we start building."

Karen had a look of determination settling on her features. "I'll organize the volunteers. And John... thank you for listening."

John smiled at her, a small but genuine smile that spoke of his gratitude for her support. "We're in this together, Karen. We'll get through it together."

With that, they turned and walked back toward the command center, ready to begin the next phase of their journey. The memorial would be the first step in a long and difficult process, but it was a step that had to be taken. For the dead, for the living, and for the future of the nation they were trying to rebuild.

Chapter 15: A Fragile Peace

The sky over the capital was a somber gray as John stood on the steps of the temporary government headquarters. The building, a sturdy but uninspired structure hastily erected from salvaged materials, served as the new heart of what remained of the United States government. It was a far cry from the grandeur of the old Capitol, but it was functional, and that was what they needed now.

As John looked out over the streets, he could see the first signs of life returning to the battered city. The roads, once choked with debris and abandoned vehicles, were now being cleared by teams of workers. Buildings that had escaped the worst of the devastation were being repaired, and makeshift markets had sprung up where survivors traded what goods they could scavenge. It was a fragile semblance of normalcy, but it was a start.

The nation was beginning to stabilize, but the scars of the war were still raw. There was a sense of unease that hung over the population, a lingering fear that the fragile peace could shatter at any moment. The tensions that had simmered beneath the surface during the worst of the crisis had not disappeared; they had merely shifted, taking on new forms as the survivors tried to rebuild their lives.

General Moore approached, his expression grim, but there was a hint of something else in his eyes—something like hope. He had been instrumental in maintaining order during the chaos, and his presence was a steadying force for both the military and the civilian population.

"Mr. President," Moore said, offering a curt nod. "The latest reports from the governors are coming in. We're seeing signs of recovery in some areas—agriculture, small-scale manufacturing, even some local economies are starting to function again."

John replied with a slight and quick smile, his gaze still on the city below. "That's good news, General. But we both know that recovery is just the first step. We've stabilized the nation for now, but we're still walking on a knife's edge. Any misstep, any breach in unity, could bring everything crashing down again."

Moore's expression hardened. "We've got a long road ahead of us, Mr. President. The war may be over, but the fight to rebuild this nation is just beginning. We're dealing with more than just physical damage. The psychological toll, the breakdown of trust and authority—those are battles we're going to be fighting for years, maybe decades."

John turned to face Moore, his eyes reflecting the weight of responsibility he felt. "How do we maintain unity, General? How do we keep this fragile coalition together when so many forces are still pulling us apart?"

Moore took a deep breath, considering his words carefully. "We need to focus on two things: stability and trust. People need to believe that the government can protect them, that we can provide for their basic needs. At the same time, we have to be transparent, honest about the challenges we're facing. The more we involve the population in the rebuilding process, the more invested they'll be in its success."

John quickly replied. "And what about the economy? We're starting to see some signs of recovery, but it's fragile at best.

If we can't get the infrastructure back online, if we can't create jobs, we risk losing whatever progress we've made."

"The infrastructure is our biggest challenge right now," Moore agreed. "We're prioritizing the most critical repairs—power grids, water supplies, transportation networks—but we're stretched thin. We need to be strategic about where we allocate resources. And we need to be prepared for setbacks. There will be regions that don't recover as quickly as others, and that's going to create tension."

John sighed, rubbing his temples. "It feels like we're trying to hold back a tidal wave with a sandbag. Every time we make progress in one area, another crisis pops up. How do we build something lasting when the foundations are still so shaky?"

Moore placed a hand on John's shoulder, his voice firm. "We take it one day at a time, Mr. President. We've come this far because we didn't give up when things seemed impossible. We can't afford to give up now."

John looked at Moore, drawing strength from the general's resolve. He knew that they were in this together, and that

Moore would be by his side no matter how difficult the road ahead became.

"Let's focus on what we can do," John said, his voice steady. "We'll keep pushing forward with the reconstruction, but we also need to invest in the future. Education, innovation—those are the things that will give us a foundation to build on. We need to give people hope, something to strive for beyond mere survival."

Moore replied. "Agreed. And we need to keep strengthening our alliances with the regional leaders. Some of them are still wary of federal authority, but if we can show them that we're all working toward the same goal, we can start to rebuild that trust."

John turned back to the city, his gaze thoughtful. "We'll start by meeting with the governors again. We need to keep those lines of communication open and make sure everyone's on the same page. And we need to be prepared to make some hard decisions. There's no room for ego in this. We have to do what's best for the nation as a whole."

Moore gave a sharp nod. "I'll coordinate with the military on logistics and security. We've already got teams working on rebuilding key infrastructure points, and I'll make sure they're supported. We'll also need to keep an eye on rogue factions—they're still a threat, especially in the more isolated regions."

John clenched his fists, a fire burning in his chest. "We'll do whatever it takes, General. We've come too far to let this nation fall apart now. We'll rebuild, we'll recover, and we'll come out of this stronger than before."

As they stood together on the steps of the government headquarters, the sky darkening with the approach of evening, John felt a renewed sense of purpose. The road ahead was fraught with challenges, but he knew that they had the strength and the will to overcome them. The nation was beginning to stabilize, but the real work of rebuilding was just beginning. And with General Moore at his side, John was determined to see it through to the end.

Chapter 16: The New Military

The war room was tense, filled with the muffled sounds of distant construction and the hum of electronic equipment. John, now weary but resolute, sat at the head of a long table, surrounded by his closest advisors. General Moore, ever the stoic figure, was on his right, while Karen sat to his left, her expression thoughtful but determined.

The topic of the day was one that had been looming over them since the first signs of stabilization—the reorganization of the U.S. military in a world that had been irrevocably altered by nuclear war. The military had been the backbone of the nation's survival, holding the fractured pieces together in the chaos that followed the bombs. But now, as they began the process of rebuilding, the role of the military had to be reconsidered.

John leaned forward with his hands clasped together on the table. "We've come a long way, but there's no denying that the world has changed. The military is no longer just a force of defense; it's become integral to our government and our society. We need to decide how we're going to adapt to this new reality."

General Moore nodded. "The military has been the stabilizing force in the aftermath, but we're entering a new phase now. Reconstruction is underway, and as much as we've relied on the military to maintain order, we need to ensure that we don't slide into a militarized state. Our focus should be on rebuilding civilian institutions."

Karen's brow furrowed as she glanced between the two men, her brow furrowed. "The balance of power is delicate right now. People trust the military because it's kept them safe, but we need to start shifting that trust back to civilian leadership. The last thing we want is for the public to see the military as the only legitimate authority."

The room fell into a heavy silence as they all considered the implications. The debate over the military's role in governance and reconstruction was not a new one, but it had taken on new urgency as the nation began to stabilize.

John broke the silence with a firm voice. "We need to reorganize the military, not just to maintain peace and security, but to support the reconstruction efforts in a way that doesn't overshadow civilian governance. We need a clear separation of powers, but we also need to be realistic about the situation we're in. The military can't just go back to its pre-war role—not yet, at least."

Moore shifted in his seat, his gaze steady. "We've already started restructuring our forces, focusing on regional command centers that can respond quickly to any threats. We've also integrated more engineering and logistical units to support reconstruction. But the question is, how do we balance that with the need to restore civilian authority?"

Karen leaned forward and spoke with a thoughtful tone. "What if we reframe the military's role as a transitional force? They could focus on stabilizing regions until civilian governments are fully functional. We could set up a timeline for transitioning authority back to civilian leadership, with clear milestones along the way."

John replied after considering the suggestion. "That makes sense. The military can continue to provide security and support for rebuilding efforts, but with a clear mandate to hand over control as civilian institutions come back online.

It'll be a balancing act, but it's one we must manage carefully."

Moore cleared his throat and responded with a serious tone. "There's also the issue of how we're going to handle dissent. We've already seen pockets of resistance—people who distrust the government and the military alike. We need to be prepared for the possibility that some regions might refuse to transition back to civilian control."

John's expression hardened. "We can't allow the country to fracture any further. If we're going to rebuild, we need to be united. That means we must find a way to maintain peace and security without resorting to heavy-handed tactics. We need to win hearts and minds, not just impose order by force."

Karen spoke up in a voice tinged with concern. "We also need to address the public perception of the military. If people start seeing the military as a permanent governing force, it could undermine everything we're trying to achieve. We need to make it clear that the military's role is temporary and that our goal is to return to civilian governance."

John looked at Moore firmly. "We need a strategy that balances all of this. The military needs to be seen as a protector, not a ruler. We'll need to communicate this clearly to the public, and we'll need to be transparent about our plans for the transition. At the same time, we must ensure that the military has the resources and authority it needs to keep the peace during this delicate period."

Moore replied with his expression resolute. "I'll work with my commanders to develop a phased plan for transitioning control back to civilian authorities. We'll also increase our efforts to engage with local leaders and communities, to build trust and cooperation."

Karen added, "And we should consider setting up joint civilian-military councils in the most sensitive regions. This could help ease the transition and ensure that civilian voices are heard in the decision-making process."

John felt a sense of clarity as the pieces began to fall into place. "Let's move forward with that plan. We'll reorganize the military to support reconstruction while laying the groundwork for a return to civilian governance. We'll communicate our intentions clearly to the public and work to build trust every step of the way."

As the meeting continued, the conversation shifted to logistics—how to allocate resources, how to prioritize regions for reconstruction, and how to handle potential hotspots of resistance. The details were complex, but John felt a renewed sense of purpose. They were not just rebuilding a nation; they were reshaping it for a new world.

Later, as the meeting adjourned and the room began to empty, Karen remained behind with John. She looked at him with a mixture of concern and admiration. "You're carrying a lot on your shoulders, John. I just want you to know that you don't have to do it alone. We're all in this together."

John smiled faintly, the weight of the day still pressing on him. "I know, Karen. And I'm grateful for that. We've all lost so much, but we've also gained something—something stronger. We're building a new world, and we're doing it together."

Karen reached out, placing a reassuring hand on his arm. "And we'll get through this, John. One step at a time."

John smiled with a firm resolve. "One step at a time."

As they left the war room together, the future of the nation still uncertain, John knew that the challenges ahead would be immense. But with the right people by his side, he believed that they could overcome them. The reorganization of the military was just the beginning of a long journey toward recovery and renewal—a journey that would define the future of the United States and the world.

Chapter 17: The New Dawn

The sun rose slowly over the horizon, casting a golden light over the landscape that had once been a thriving city but was now a mixture of ruins and reconstruction. In the heart of the emerging new capital, the air buzzed with the sound of hammers and saws as workers toiled to rebuild what had been lost. Yet, amid the labor of reconstruction, there was something new in the air—an energy, a spirit that had been absent in the bleak days following the nuclear war. It was the return of culture, the rebirth of the arts, music, and traditions that had long defined the American spirit.

The President stood on the balcony of his temporary headquarters, watching as a group of children played in the open square below. Laughter echoed through the streets, a sound that had been scarce in recent months. Beside the children, a woman strummed a guitar, her fingers coaxing a melody that seemed to float on the breeze, carrying with it a sense of hope.

John smiled faintly, turning to his Vice President, who joined him on the balcony. "It's good to see this," he said softly. "The return of something... normal."

Her eyes took in the scene below. "It's more than just normal, John. It's a sign that we're beginning to heal. People are starting to express themselves again, to find meaning in the midst of all this. It's a crucial step in rebuilding not just our infrastructure, but our society."

The return of cultural life had been gradual, like the first green shoots emerging from the scorched earth. At first, it had been small things—a song hummed while working, a child drawing with a piece of charcoal on the sidewalk. But as the weeks passed, these small acts of creativity began to grow, spreading like wildfire through the surviving communities. Music, art, and storytelling began to take root once more, bringing with them a sense of identity and continuity that had been all but lost in the chaos.

John knew that this resurgence of culture was essential for the nation's recovery. Without it, they were just rebuilding buildings and roads, but not the soul of the country. "We've focused so much on survival, on the physical rebuilding,"

John said with a thoughtful voice. "But we can't lose sight of what makes us who we are. Our culture, our traditions—they're what bind us together as a nation. We need to nurture that."

Karen smiled at him with a hint of pride in her eyes. "And we are. Schools are reopening, universities are being re-established. Cultural institutions are beginning to take shape again. It's slow, but it's happening."

The re-establishment of schools and universities had been one of the administration's top priorities. Education was the foundation upon which the future would be built, and John had pushed hard to ensure that it was given the attention it deserved. Schools had started reopening in the safer zones, staffed by teachers who were often as traumatized as the students they taught, but determined to give them the knowledge and hope they needed to face the future. Universities, too, were beginning to emerge from the ashes, albeit in a more modest form than before. Makeshift campuses sprang up in repurposed buildings, where the brightest minds gathered to share knowledge and ideas.

It wasn't just the old ways that were returning. New philosophies and ways of thinking were emerging, born from the shared trauma of the war and the need to find meaning in a world that had been turned upside down. Communities were coming together, not just to rebuild their homes, but to redefine what it meant to be part of the United States in this new era. Debates over ethics, governance, and human nature became as common as discussions about food and shelter.

John was acutely aware of the significance of these developments. As much as they needed to rebuild the physical structures of their society, they also needed to rebuild its intellectual and spiritual foundations. "People are rethinking everything," he said, turning to Karen. "What it means to be American, what our values are, how we relate to each other and to the world. This is a chance for us to create something better out of the ruins."

Karen's gaze was steady. "And what's your vision for that future, John? What do you see for the United States?"

John paused, taking a deep breath as he gathered his thoughts. "I see a nation that's stronger for what it's been through, but also more compassionate. A place where we don't just rebuild what was lost, but where we build something better. Where our diversity is our strength, and where we learn from our past mistakes to create a society that's just, equitable, and sustainable."

Karen nodded slowly, absorbing his words. "That's a powerful vision. And I believe it's one that people will rally behind. But it won't be easy. There are still so many challenges ahead."

John's expression hardened with determination. "I know. But we can't afford to shy away from those challenges. If we do, we'll just be repeating the same mistakes that led us to this point. We have to push forward, to make the hard decisions now so that future generations have a chance at a better life."

The challenges were indeed daunting. Re-establishing cultural institutions was a monumental task, not least because of the scarcity of resources. The nation's economy was still in shambles, and many people were focused solely on survival. But John knew that if they didn't invest in the cultural and intellectual life of the nation, they would lose something far more important than physical infrastructure.

"Art, music, literature—they're what give life meaning," John continued. "We need to support our artists, our thinkers, our educators. They're the ones who will help us make sense of everything that's happened and guide us toward a better future."

Karen smiled warmly. "You're right. And we will. We'll make sure that the arts and education are given the priority they deserve. It's not just about surviving anymore; it's about thriving."

"Exactly", John said with a firm resolve. "We have to look to the future, to create a society that's not just rebuilt, but reimagined. One that's worthy of the sacrifices that have been made."

As they stood there, watching the children play and listening to the music that filled the air, John felt a renewed sense of hope. The road ahead was long and fraught with challenges, but he knew that they were on the right path. With the gradual return of cultural life, the reopening of schools and universities, and the emergence of new ways of thinking, they were beginning to build a future that was not just a continuation of the past, but something entirely new.

In the weeks that followed, John and Karen spearheaded the creation of several initiatives aimed at fostering this cultural revival. They worked closely with community leaders, educators, and artists to establish a series of workshops and cultural centers in the new capital. These centers served as hubs of creativity, where people could come together to share their stories, express their emotions, and reconnect with the cultural heritage that had been nearly lost.

One of the first projects was the creation of a national memorial to honor the lives lost in the war. It was a massive undertaking, both logistically and emotionally, but John knew it was necessary. The memorial would serve not only as a place of remembrance but also as a symbol of resilience and hope for the future.

Construction of the memorial began in the heart of the capital, on a site that had once been a bustling city square. The plans called for a vast open space surrounded by walls etched with the names of the fallen. At the center, a towering sculpture would rise, symbolizing the strength and unity of the nation in the face of unimaginable loss. The design was chosen from submissions by artists across the country, reflecting the collaborative spirit that John was determined to foster.

As the memorial began to take shape, so too did the cultural revival that John had envisioned. Schools and universities continued to reopen, with new curricula that reflected the changed world. Courses on history, ethics, and philosophy were reimagined to include lessons learned from the war, while the arts flourished as a means of healing and expression.

In the evenings, the people of the capital would gather in the square around the memorial, listening to concerts, watching plays, and participating in discussions about the future of the nation. The square became a living symbol of the rebirth of culture, a place where the past was honored and the future was forged.

One night, as John and Karen stood together watching a performance in the square, Karen turned to him with a thoughtful look. "Do you think they'll understand, John? The people, I mean. Do you think they'll understand why we're putting so much emphasis on this, on culture and education, when there are still so many other urgent needs?"

John looked at her, his face illuminated by the soft glow of the lights around the square. "I think they will, eventually. Right now, survival is still the most pressing concern for many, but we can't lose sight of the bigger picture. Without culture, without education, we're just rebuilding shells. We need to rebuild the soul of this nation, too. And that takes time, patience, and a lot of hard work. But it's worth it."

Her eyes reflected the determination she saw in John. "You're right. And we won't give up. This is too important."

As the performance continued, John found himself thinking about the future. The road ahead was still uncertain, with many challenges yet to be faced. But for the first time in a long while, he felt a sense of hope, a belief that they could build something new and enduring from the ashes of the old world.

In the months that followed, the cultural revival continued to gain momentum. More and more people began to participate in the arts, to express themselves in ways that had been stifled during the dark days of the war. Music filled the streets, paintings and murals adorned the walls of the new buildings, and storytelling became a way to preserve the collective memory of what had been lost and what had been found.

The reopening of schools and universities played a crucial role in this cultural renaissance. Educators, many of whom had lost their own families in the war, were determined to give the next generation the tools they needed to rebuild and reimagine their world. New courses were developed, focusing on everything from sustainable agriculture and renewable energy to peace studies and conflict resolution. These courses reflected the new realities of the post-apocalyptic world, as well as the lessons that had been learned from the mistakes of the past.

John made a point of visiting these educational institutions whenever he could, speaking with students and teachers, listening to their concerns, and offering his support. He knew that the future of the nation depended on these young minds, and he was committed to giving them every opportunity to succeed.

One day, while visiting a newly established university in the capital, John was approached by a group of students who wanted to share their ideas for the future of the country. They spoke passionately about the need for greater emphasis on environmental sustainability, on social justice, and on creating a society that valued human dignity above all else. John listened intently, encouraged by their enthusiasm and their vision for a better world.

"We're not just rebuilding what was lost," one of the students said, her voice filled with conviction. "We're building something new, something better. And we have the chance to do it right this time."

John smiled, feeling a deep sense of pride. "You're absolutely right. And it's up to all of us to make sure that we don't squander this opportunity. We have to work together, to learn from each other, and to build a future that honors the sacrifices that have been made."

As he walked away from the university that day, John couldn't help but feel a renewed sense of purpose. The challenges ahead were still immense, but he knew that they were on the right path. The cultural revival, the reopening of schools and universities, the emergence of new philosophies and ways of thinking—these were all signs that the nation was beginning to heal, to find its way forward.

And in the center of it all, the memorial continued to rise, a towering symbol of the resilience and determination of the American people. It was a reminder of the past, of the lives that had been lost, but also a beacon of hope for the future. As the final pieces of the sculpture were put into place, John and Karen stood together in the square, watching as the workers completed their task.

"It's beautiful," Karen said softly, her voice filled with emotion. "A fitting tribute to everyone we've lost."

John's eyes fixed on the memorial. "It's more than just a tribute, Karen. It's a promise. A promise that we will remember and that we will honor their sacrifice by building something better. And that we will never forget what brought us to this point."

As they stood there, watching the sun set behind the memorial, John felt a deep sense of peace. The road ahead was still uncertain, with many challenges yet to be faced. But for the first time in a long while, he felt a sense of hope, a belief that they could build something new and enduring from the ashes of the old world. The nation was beginning to heal, to find its way forward, and with it, the soul of the country was being reborn.

This was the beginning of a new chapter in the history of the United States, one that would be defined not by the devastation of the past, but by the hope and determination of its people to build a better future. And in that future, John saw the possibility of a nation that had not just survived the apocalypse, but had risen from its ashes stronger, wiser, and more united than ever before.

Chapter 18: The Foreign Threat

The tension in the air was palpable, a subtle yet persistent reminder that something was amiss. John had grown accustomed to the quiet before a storm, but this time, the storm felt different—darker, more ominous. The first signs of trouble came from the intelligence reports. A cryptic message intercepted by one of their still-functioning satellites suggested unusual activity in a foreign territory. John's instincts told him that it was more than just a coincidence.

The situation quickly escalated when reports began flooding in about military movements in regions that had remained relatively stable after the nuclear devastation. The Atlantic coast, already vulnerable and sparsely defended, became the focus of concern as foreign naval fleets were detected moving closer to U.S. waters. John convened an emergency meeting with his top advisors in the newly established war room.

The war room, hastily set up in a repurposed underground facility, was dimly lit by the soft glow of screens displaying satellite images, intelligence reports, and communication logs. The room hummed with low murmurs as generals, diplomats, and advisors reviewed the latest developments. General Moore stood at the head of the table, his expression as grim as ever. The map on the central screen showed the positions of foreign fleets moving closer to the U.S. coastline.

"They're testing us," General Moore began, his voice cutting through the silence. "They see us as weak and vulnerable after everything that's happened. They think now's the time to push, to see how far they can go before we push back."

John studied the map, his mind racing through potential scenarios. "What's our current military readiness?"

Moore hesitated which was a sign that John had learned to dread. "We're operating at a fraction of our pre-war capacity. We've salvaged some of our nuclear deterrents, and we've managed to re-establish contact with several military bases. But conventional forces are spread thin, and supplies—especially fuel and ammunition—are critically low. We can defend, but not without significant risk."

John took a deep breath. The nation was still reeling from the aftershocks of the nuclear war, and now it faced the very real threat of foreign aggression. The room felt colder, as if the gravity of the situation had seeped into the walls.

Karen, seated beside John, leaned forward. "Diplomatically, we're isolated," she said, her voice steady despite the tension. "Most of our traditional allies are dealing with their own crises, and our enemies see us as easy prey. We need to act carefully. One wrong move, and we could be facing a full-scale invasion."

Processing the information, John knew the decision ahead was monumental. The United States, though weakened, was still a nation of resilience, and he had no intention of letting it fall further into chaos.

"We need to send a message," John said with a firm voice. "General, prepare our forces for a defensive posture. We must show strength without provoking an outright conflict. Karen, reach out to what's left of our alliances. We need to present a united front, even if it's just for show. And send a message to this foreign power: We're willing to talk, but any further aggression will be met with force."

The plan was set into motion with urgency. Across the eastern seaboard, military units scrambled to reinforce key defensive positions, while diplomats worked tirelessly to open channels with allies and potential adversaries alike. The airwaves crackled with coded messages, and the nation held its breath, waiting for what would come next.

Despite the heightened tension, the nights were eerily quiet. John often found himself alone in the war room, staring at the screens that displayed the latest intelligence. His thoughts drifted to the past, to the days before the war, when the world was a different place. He had made countless decisions as president, but none had weighed as heavily as the ones he faced now.

Karen joined him one night, the two of them standing side by side, watching the map as it tracked the foreign fleets. "We've been through hell and back," she said softly. "But this… this feels different."

"It does," John replied, his voice tinged with the fatigue of leadership. "We're not just fighting for survival anymore. We're fighting for the future."

As the days passed, the situation grew increasingly dire. The foreign power, emboldened by what it perceived as American weakness, began making more aggressive moves. Skirmishes broke out along the coast, small engagements that tested the resolve of the U.S. forces. Each encounter brought the threat of escalation, and John knew that the country was on a knife's edge.

In the war room, General Moore outlined the latest developments. "Their fleet is moving closer to our eastern defenses. If they push any further, we'll have no choice but to engage them directly. Our forces are ready, but we're running out of time."

John's mind raced, weighing the options. He knew that any misstep could lead to disaster, but inaction would be equally dangerous. The nation could not afford another war, yet it could not allow itself to be bullied into submission.

"Prepare a show of force," John ordered. "Deploy our fleet to intercept them, and make sure they know we're serious.

At the same time, we continue pushing for negotiations. We need to avoid conflict, but we can't let them think we're weak."

Moore agreed, immediately setting the plan into motion. The war room buzzed with activity as orders were relayed, and military units moved into position. The nation held its breath, waiting to see whether diplomacy or war would prevail.

In the midst of the crisis, John took a moment to address the American people. Broadcasting from the war room, he spoke with the calm authority that had become his hallmark. "We are a nation that has faced unimaginable challenges," he began. "We have endured loss, suffering, and devastation, but we have also shown resilience, strength, and unity. Today, we face a new challenge, a foreign power that seeks to exploit our perceived weakness. Let me be clear: We will defend our land, our people, and our way of life. We seek peace, but we are prepared for whatever may come."

The response was immediate. Across the nation, communities rallied, civilians volunteering to support the military effort in any way they could. Supplies were gathered, defenses were fortified, and the spirit of resistance that had carried the country through the nuclear fallout began to stir once more.

John watched the developments with a mixture of pride and concern. The nation was rising to the challenge, but he knew that the worst was yet to come. The foreign power showed no signs of backing down, and the threat of a full-scale invasion loomed larger with each passing day.

The turning point came when a critical intelligence report landed on John's desk. The foreign power had deployed additional forces, and their intentions were clear: they were preparing for an attack. John convened another emergency meeting with his advisors, the atmosphere in the war room tense and focused.

"They're going to strike soon," Moore said, his voice heavy with the weight of the situation. "If we don't act now, we could lose the eastern seaboard."

John's heart pounded as he absorbed the gravity of the moment. This was it—the decision that could determine the fate of the nation.

"Moore, prepare for a limited strike," John ordered, his voice resolute. "Target their naval base. We need to show them that we won't be intimidated, but we can't afford to start a full-blown war. Karen, double down on our diplomatic efforts. Use this show of force to push them to the negotiating table."

The room erupted into action as the orders were carried out. John stood in the center of it all, his mind racing with the implications of what was about to unfold. This was a gamble—a calculated risk that could either de-escalate the situation or plunge the nation into a new conflict.

Hours later, the strike was executed with precision. U.S. forces launched a barrage of missiles at the foreign naval base, destroying key installations and crippling their ability to launch an immediate counterattack. The message was clear: the United States was not as weakened as it appeared.

The foreign power, shocked by the unexpected show of strength, hesitated. Diplomatic channels, which had been fraught with tension, suddenly opened up, and the possibility of a ceasefire became real. Karen and her team worked tirelessly to broker a deal, using the strike as leverage to bring the foreign power to the negotiating table.

As the situation began to stabilize, John felt a sense of cautious relief. The nation had avoided a disaster, but the scars of the crisis would linger. The experience had tested not only the country's military capabilities but also its resilience and unity.

In the days that followed, John reflected on the journey that had brought them to this point. The country had come perilously close to the edge, but it had held together, thanks in no small part to the determination of its people. The foreign threat had been neutralized, but the road ahead remained uncertain. The nation had survived the latest crisis, but John knew that there were still challenges to come.

As he looked out over the rebuilding capital, John made a silent vow to himself and to the country he had sworn to protect. The United States would rise from the ashes, stronger and more united than ever before. This was not the end—it was a new beginning. And he would lead them through it, no matter the cost.

The stage was set for the final reckoning, where the ultimate test of leadership and resilience awaited.

Chapter 19: The Final Reckoning

The dawn broke over the battered landscape, casting long shadows across the ruined cityscape of Washington, D.C. The nation had weathered the storm of foreign aggression, but John knew that the greatest challenge was still ahead. The recent conflict had only deepened the fractures within the country, and the fragile peace was in danger of unraveling. As the sun rose, so too did the specter of a new crisis—one that could undo all the progress they had fought so hard to achieve.

John stood at the window of his temporary office, watching as the first light of day spread across the horizon. The capital was still a shell of its former self, but there were signs of life returning. Construction crews worked tirelessly to rebuild the city, soldiers patrolled the streets, and the people began to tentatively reclaim their lives. Yet, beneath the surface, there was an undercurrent of unease. The nation had been pushed to its limits, and the stress fractures were beginning to show.

The situation came to a head when a series of coordinated attacks rocked the country. It started with sabotage at key infrastructure sites—power plants, water treatment facilities, and communication hubs were all targeted. The nation, already struggling to regain its footing, was thrown into chaos once again. Panic spread as rumors of insurrection and civil war began to circulate. The very fabric of the country seemed to be unraveling.

John immediately called an emergency meeting with his top advisors. The atmosphere in the war room was tense, the air thick with the weight of the decisions that had to be made. General Moore was the first to speak, his voice gruff and determined.

"We've confirmed that these attacks were coordinated by a domestic insurgent group," Moore reported. "They're well-organized and well-armed, and they've managed to rally a significant portion of the population to their cause. They're not just trying to disrupt—they're trying to overthrow the government."

The words hung in the air like a death sentence. John's heart sank as he realized the full extent of the threat. This was no mere rebellion—it was a full-scale uprising, one that threatened to tear the nation apart at its seams.

"Who are they?" John asked, his voice calm but laced with urgency. "What do they want?"

Karen, who had been quietly reviewing intelligence reports, looked up and met John's gaze. "They call themselves the New American Federation," she said, her tone somber. "Their leaders are former military officers and political figures who believe that the current government has failed. They want to establish a new order, one that's based on their vision of a 'purified' America—one that's strong, authoritarian, and completely free from foreign influence."

The implications were chilling. This group represented the darkest impulses of the post-apocalyptic world—fear, hatred, and the desire for absolute control. If they succeeded, the United States as John knew it would cease to exist.

"We need to act fast," John said, his mind racing through the options. "We can't let them gain any more ground.

Moore, I want a full assessment of their capabilities and a plan to neutralize them. Karen, reach out to our allies and regional leaders. We need to present a united front against this threat."

The room buzzed with activity as orders were relayed and plans were drawn up. But even as the preparations began, John knew that this would be the most difficult battle yet. The enemy was not a foreign power, but fellow Americans—people who, in their own twisted way, believed they were fighting for the country's future.

As the hours turned into days, the situation grew increasingly dire. The New American Federation launched a series of brazen attacks, seizing control of several key cities and declaring themselves the rightful government. Their propaganda spread like wildfire, sowing seeds of doubt and fear among the population. John's administration, already stretched thin, struggled to contain the growing insurgency.

In the midst of the chaos, John found himself facing a crisis of confidence. The weight of leadership had never felt heavier, and the toll of the past months began to wear on him. The loss of his family, the constant threats to the nation, and the knowledge that he was now fighting his own people—all of it threatened to overwhelm him.

One evening, as the country teetered on the brink of civil war, Karen found John alone in his office. He was staring out the window, his expression unreadable. She had seen him in many states—determined, resolute, even vulnerable—but never like this. There was a weariness in his eyes that spoke of a man on the edge.

"John," Karen said softly, stepping into the room. "You've been through more than anyone should ever have to endure. But the country needs you now more than ever. You can't give up."

John turned to face her, his voice tinged with despair. "I don't know if I have anything left to give, Karen. We've come so far, but now it feels like we're right back where we started. How do I ask people to keep fighting when I'm not even sure we can win?"

Karen stepped closer, her expression one of compassion and resolve. "Because they believe in you, John. You've led them through the darkest times, and they trust you to lead them out of this one too. We've faced impossible odds before, and we've come out stronger. This is no different. You have to find the strength to keep going—not just for yourself, but for all of us."

John looked at her, the weight of her words sinking in. He knew she was right. He couldn't afford to falter now, not when the stakes were so high. The nation was depending on him, and he had to rise to the occasion, no matter how impossible it seemed.

Drawing on a reserve of inner strength, John made a decision. "We need to take the fight to them," he said, his voice firm with renewed determination. "We can't just defend—we have to go on the offensive. Moore, I want you to coordinate a series of strategic strikes against their strongholds. We need to cut off their leadership and disrupt their operations. Karen, work with the regional leaders to rally support. We need to show the country that we're still in control."

The plan was bold, risky even, but it was their best chance to turn the tide. The following days were a blur of action and tension as the administration launched a full-scale effort to suppress the rebellion. The military strikes were surgical and devastating, targeting the insurgent command centers and supply lines. Meanwhile, Karen and her team worked tirelessly to counter the insurgents' propaganda, broadcasting messages of unity and resilience.

The nation held its breath as the conflict reached its climax. Battles raged across the country, with loyalist forces clashing with the New American Federation in a desperate struggle for control. The outcome was uncertain, and the cost in lives was steep. But slowly, the tide began to turn. The insurgents, caught off guard by the ferocity of the government's response, began to lose ground.

Amid the fighting, John made a rare public appearance, speaking directly to the American people. His voice, though weary, was filled with conviction. "We have faced unimaginable trials," he said, "but we have not broken. We will not allow those who seek to divide us to succeed. This is our country, our home, and we will fight for it with everything we have. We will rebuild, we will recover, and we will emerge stronger than ever."

The speech had a galvanizing effect, rallying the population and bolstering the morale of the loyalist forces. The insurgents, realizing that their cause was doomed, began to splinter, with some factions surrendering and others attempting to flee. The government's victory, while hard-fought and costly, was finally within reach.

As the dust began to settle, John knew that the real work was just beginning. The nation had survived yet another existential threat, but the scars of the conflict would linger. There would be no easy path to recovery, but the foundations had been laid.

In the aftermath of the uprising, John and Karen walked through the devastated streets of the capital, surveying the damage. The city, though battered and bruised, was still standing—a testament to the resilience of its people.

"We did it," Karen said quietly, her voice tinged with both relief and sorrow.

John looked down towards the cracked pavement below them with a dull expression. "We did. But at what cost? So much has been lost, and there's still so much to do."

Karen placed a hand on his shoulder, offering a comforting smile. "We'll rebuild, John. We've come through the worst of it, and now we have a chance to start anew. The country needs your vision, your leadership. And I'll be right there with you, every step of the way."

John looked at her, grateful for her unwavering support. Together, they had faced the darkest days of the nation's history, and together, they would lead the way into a brighter future.

The nation's response to the final reckoning was one of cautious optimism. The people, exhausted by the years of conflict and hardship, were ready for peace and stability. The government, under John's leadership, began the arduous process of healing the wounds of division and rebuilding the shattered remains of the country.

In the weeks that followed, John and Karen worked tirelessly to lay the groundwork for a new chapter in the nation's history. The insurgents were disbanded, their leaders brought to justice, and efforts were made to reintegrate their followers into society. The military, though stretched thin, remained a crucial force for maintaining order and security.

The economy, slowly but surely, began to recover, as trade routes were reestablished and industries started to rebuild. Infrastructure projects, aimed at restoring the nation's critical systems, were launched with renewed vigor. Schools and universities reopened their doors, and cultural life began to stir once more.

As the country moved forward, John remained a steady presence, guiding the nation with a vision of hope and resilience. He knew that the road ahead would be long and difficult, but he also knew that they had the strength to endure. The United States, though changed forever by the trials it had faced, would not only survive—it would thrive.

Chapter 20: The Legacy of Leadership

As the final months of John's presidency began to unfold, the weight of the past couple years hung heavily on his shoulders. The nation had come a long way from the brink of annihilation, but the scars of war were still fresh, both on the land and in the hearts of the people. Each day brought new challenges and decisions, yet with the end of his term drawing nearer, John found himself increasingly reflective, pondering the legacy he would leave behind.

The sun was setting over the rebuilt Washington, D.C., casting long shadows across the city that had once been the seat of power for a nation now forever changed. John stood in his temporary office, a makeshift Oval Office in a secure facility, as the original White House remained under reconstruction. The room, though practical, lacked the grandeur of its predecessor, a reminder of the ongoing struggle to rebuild not just structures, but the very fabric of the nation.

John's thoughts drifted back to the beginning of his presidency, to the day when the world had changed in an instant. The nuclear war had decimated cities, shattered lives, and left the United States a fractured and fragile shell of its former self. But through sheer determination and the unwavering support of a dedicated team, John had managed to hold the country together, guiding it through the storm.

As he gazed out the window at the rebuilding capital, John knew that the transition of power would be one of the most critical moments in the nation's recovery. The United States was still fragile, its democracy tenuous, and the peaceful transfer of leadership was not just a formality—it was a test of the country's resilience and its ability to endure in a changed world.

John had always believed in the power of institutions, in the strength of a government built on principles rather than personalities. But the reality of the post-apocalyptic world had forced him to adapt, to be more than just a leader of a government—he had become a symbol of survival, of hope, and of the possibility of a future. Now, as his term neared its end, he felt the enormous responsibility of ensuring that the next leader would be capable of carrying that torch.

One of John's primary concerns was the future of leadership in the United States. The nation had been rebuilt on the shoulders of those who had risen to the occasion, but the next generation would need to be prepared to take on the mantle of responsibility. In his final months, John devoted considerable time to mentoring emerging leaders, individuals who had shown promise and dedication in the face of unimaginable adversity.

Emily Carter, the young senator who had become one of John's closest confidants, was at the forefront of these efforts. John had seen in her the same qualities that had guided him through his presidency—integrity, courage, and an unwavering commitment to the nation's future. He spent countless hours with Emily, discussing the challenges she would face, the decisions she would have to make, and the lessons he had learned along the way.

During one of their many discussions, Emily asked John a question that had been on her mind for some time. "Mr. President, as you look back on everything you've done, what do you think your legacy will be? How do you want to be remembered?"

John leaned back in his chair, considering the question carefully. It was a question that every leader inevitably faced, but one that he had often pushed aside in favor of focusing on the present. Now, with the end of his term in sight, it was a question he could no longer ignore.

"I hope to be remembered as someone who did what needed to be done," John said slowly. "I made difficult choices, some of which will be debated for years to come, but I always acted with the nation's best interests at heart. My goal was never just to survive, but to rebuild, to create a foundation for a future that would be stronger than the past. If I can leave behind a country that is more united, more resilient, and more hopeful, then I'll consider my presidency a success."

Emily quickly responded after absorbing his words. "You've done more than just rebuild, sir. You've given people a reason to believe in the future again. That's a legacy that will endure."

But John knew that his legacy would be tested by the challenges that lay ahead. The United States was still fragile, its unity constantly threatened by the memories of war and the lingering fear of what might come next. The economy, though showing signs of recovery, was still vulnerable, and the social fabric of the nation had been stretched to its limits. The next leader would need to be strong, decisive, and above all, committed to the principles that had guided the nation through its darkest days.

As the weeks passed, John began to prepare for the transition of power. He held meetings with his advisors, with military leaders, and with the key figures who would play a role in the next administration. He knew that the process would be delicate, that any misstep could lead to instability, but he was determined to ensure that the nation continued to move forward, no matter who was at the helm.

In private moments, John reflected on the personal toll of his presidency. The weight of responsibility had been immense, and the decisions he had made had left him with scars that would never fully heal. He thought of his family, of the loss that had nearly broken him, and of the countless lives that had been lost under his watch. But he also thought of the people who had been saved, of the cities that were beginning to rebuild, and of the hope that was slowly returning to a nation that had once been on the brink of despair.

One evening, John sat down with Karen, who had been his steadfast ally throughout the entire ordeal. The two of them had shared the burden of leadership, and Karen had been there for John during his darkest moments. Together, they had faced the impossible, and together, they had begun to rebuild a nation.

"Karen," John said, breaking the silence that had settled between them, "I want to thank you for everything you've done. I couldn't have gotten through this without you."

Karen smiled, her expression one of deep respect and friendship. "We did this together, John. And we're not done yet."

They talked late into the night, discussing the challenges that still lay ahead, the plans for the future, and the importance of ensuring a smooth transition of power. They both knew that the next few months would be critical, not just for the administration, but for the future of the country.

As the conversation turned to more personal matters, John and Karen found themselves reflecting on their shared experiences of loss. John already knew of Karen's mother's death, a tragedy that had only deepened the bond between them. They had both suffered, both lost loved ones, but they had also found strength in each other, and in the shared responsibility of leading a nation through its darkest hour.

"Your mother would be proud of you, Karen," John said softly, recognizing the unspoken grief that still lingered between them.

"And your family would be proud of you, John," Karen replied with equal sincerity. "We've both carried a heavy burden, but we've done it together. That's something I'll always be grateful for."

Their conversation turned back to the future, to the next steps in rebuilding the country and ensuring a smooth transition of power. John knew that his time as president was nearing its end, but he also knew that his work was far from over. The nation still needed strong leadership, and he was determined to do everything in his power to ensure that the transition was successful and that the country continued to move forward.

The next chapter of the nation's story was about to begin, and John was ready to face whatever challenges lay ahead. He had spent his presidency rebuilding a nation, and now, as his time in office drew to a close, he was focused on ensuring that the legacy he left behind would be one of hope, resilience, and unity.

The road had been long and difficult, but as John looked out over the city that had been the heart of the nation for centuries, he felt a deep sense of accomplishment. The United States had been tested in ways that few could have imagined, but it had survived. And as long as there were leaders willing to step up and continue the work, he knew that the nation's future was bright.

Chapter 21: Rebirth

The world had changed, irrevocably and in ways no one could have ever imagined. The United States, once on the brink of collapse, was beginning to rise from the ashes of devastation. The journey had been long and arduous, fraught with loss and uncertainty, but as the sun began to rise on a new day, it illuminated a nation that was slowly but surely rebuilding itself—stronger, more united, and more determined than ever.

As John stepped out onto the balcony of the temporary Capitol building, the air was filled with a sense of renewal. Below him, the city of Washington, D.C., though still scarred from the war, buzzed with activity. Cranes dotted the skyline, workers tirelessly rebuilding homes, monuments, and government buildings that had been lost in the devastation. The streets, once eerily quiet, now echoed with the sounds of life as citizens returned, reclaiming their city and their future.

In the months since the final crisis that had nearly undone all they had worked for, the nation had begun to truly rebuild. New industries had emerged, born out of necessity and innovation. Renewable energy, advanced communication systems, and sustainable agriculture became the cornerstones of a new economy that was more resilient and less dependent on the fragile infrastructures of the past. Factories that had once produced weapons of war were now creating the tools of peace—machines that harnessed clean energy, devices that connected the remotest regions, and vehicles that traversed the altered landscapes with ease.

The American people, though forever changed by the horrors they had endured, displayed an enduring spirit that had become the bedrock of the nation's recovery. Communities, once isolated and distrustful, had learned to come together, to support one another, and to rebuild not just their homes but their sense of purpose. Schools and universities reopened, their halls filled with the laughter of children and the debates of scholars, all eager to shape the new world they would inherit. Arts and culture, too, began to flourish again, as people sought to express their experiences and heal through creativity.

For John, the past few months had been a time of reflection and preparation. He had seen the nation through its darkest hours and guided it toward a future that, while uncertain, was filled with possibility. Now, as his presidency neared its end, it was time to address the nation one final time.

Standing before the microphone, John looked out over the crowd that had gathered to hear his farewell speech. Thousands had come from across the country, many of them survivors who had lived through the worst of the war and were now part of the rebuilding effort. Their faces, marked by the hardships they had endured, were also filled with hope and determination.

John took a deep breath, feeling the weight of the moment. His journey as president was coming to an end, but the journey of the nation was just beginning.

"My fellow Americans," he began, his voice strong and clear, "we stand here today on the threshold of a new era. An era born from the ashes of destruction, forged in the fires of adversity, and sustained by the unbreakable spirit of the American people."

He paused, letting the words sink in. "When I took office, our nation faced challenges unlike any we had ever encountered. The devastation was overwhelming, the losses immeasurable, and the future uncertain. But through it all, we never lost hope. We never gave up. And today, because of your courage, your resilience, and your unwavering commitment to each other, we are stronger than ever before."

John's eyes scanned the crowd, meeting the gaze of those who had been with him through every step of the journey—Karen, General Moore, and countless others who had dedicated themselves to the nation's recovery.

"In the face of adversity, we came together. We rebuilt our cities, our communities, and our way of life. We harnessed the power of innovation to create new industries and technologies that will not only sustain us but propel us into the future. We reestablished our values, our traditions, and our commitment to justice and equality. And above all, we reaffirmed our belief in the enduring strength of our democracy."

The crowd erupted in applause, their cheers a testament to the truth of his words. John waited for the noise to die down before continuing.

"As I prepare to pass the torch to the next generation of leaders, I do so with the knowledge that the United States is once again a beacon of hope, not just for our citizens, but for the world. We have shown that no matter how dark the night, the dawn will always come. And with it, the promise of a new day."

John's voice softened as he reached the final part of his speech. "To those who have lost loved ones, know that their sacrifice was not in vain. Their memory lives on in every step we take toward a better future. To those who have fought for this nation, whether on the front lines or in our communities, know that your efforts have laid the foundation for the America we are building today. And to the young people of this country, know that the future is yours to shape. You are the stewards of this new world, and I have every confidence that you will lead us to even greater heights."

He paused once more, feeling the emotion of the moment. "It has been the greatest honor of my life to serve as your president. Together, we have faced the unthinkable and emerged stronger for it. Together, we have proven that the American spirit cannot be broken. And together, we will continue to build a future that is worthy of the sacrifices we have made."

As John finished his speech, the crowd rose to their feet, their applause filling the air with a sound that seemed to reverberate through the very foundations of the city. It was a sound of triumph, of resilience, and of hope.

For John, it was the perfect note on which to end his presidency. He had done what he had set out to do—to rebuild a nation that was not just surviving, but thriving. And as he stepped away from the podium, he knew that the United States was in good hands, ready to face whatever challenges the future might bring.

The nation was moving forward, stronger and more united than ever. And though John's role as president was coming to an end, his legacy would endure in the hearts and minds of the people he had served. The story of the United States was far from over, and the chapters yet to be written would be guided by the values, the vision, and the spirit that had carried them through the darkest of times.

Made in the USA
Columbia, SC
23 August 2024

5de0b97f-038f-4aba-b4be-f86ddbc441c8R01